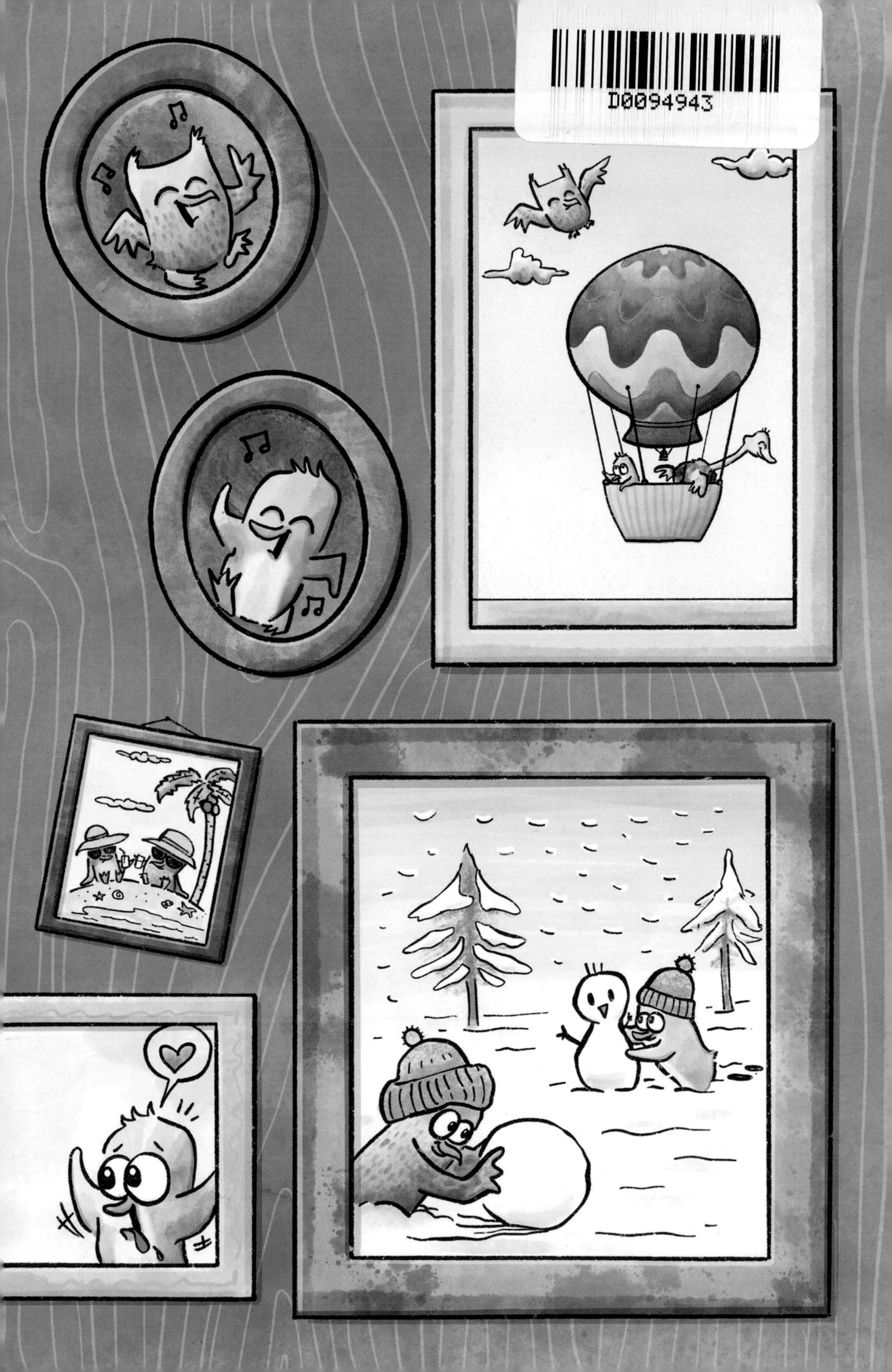

I Like to Read® Comics instill confidence and the joy of reading in new readers. Created by award-winning artists as well as talented newcomers, these imaginative books support beginners' reading comprehension with extensive visual support.

We want to hear every new reader say, "I like to read comics!"

Visit our website for flash cards,
activities, and more about the series:
www.holidayhouse.com/ILiketoRead
#ILTR

For Priya

Text and illustrations copyright © 2023 by Vikram Madan
All Rights Reserved
HOLIDAY HOUSE is registered in the U.S. Patent and Trademark Office.
Printed and bound in February 2023 at C&C Offset, Shenzhen, China.
The artwork was hand drawn on a tablet computer.
www.holidayhouse.com
First Edition
1 3 5 7 9 10 8 6 4 2

Library of Congress Cataloging-in-Publication Data is available.

ISBN: 978-0-8234-5151-7 (hardcover)

Owl and Penguin

BEST DAY EVER

Vikram Madan

HOLIDAY HOUSE · NEW YORK

PLAYTIME

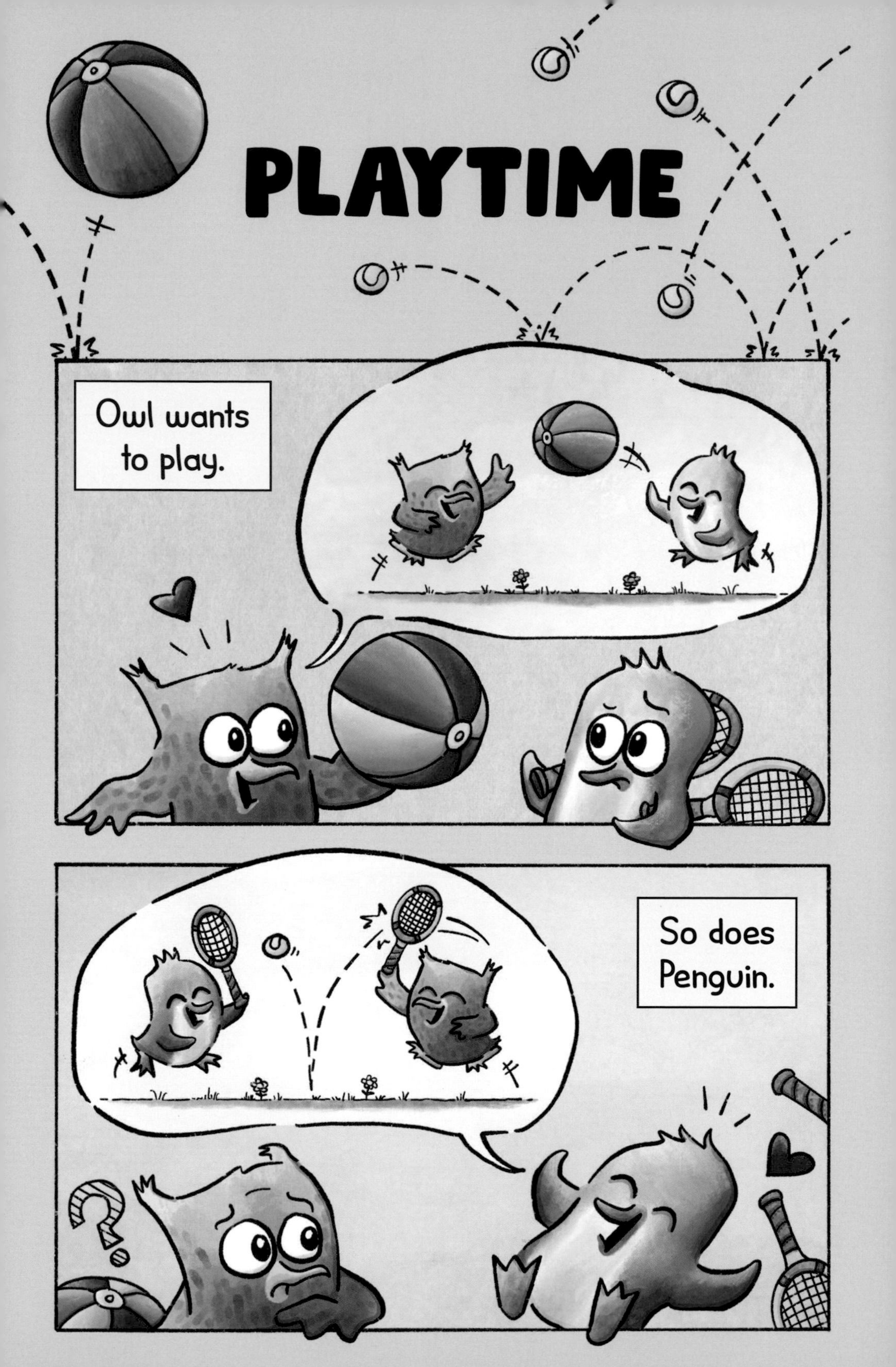
Owl wants
to play.
So does
Penguin.

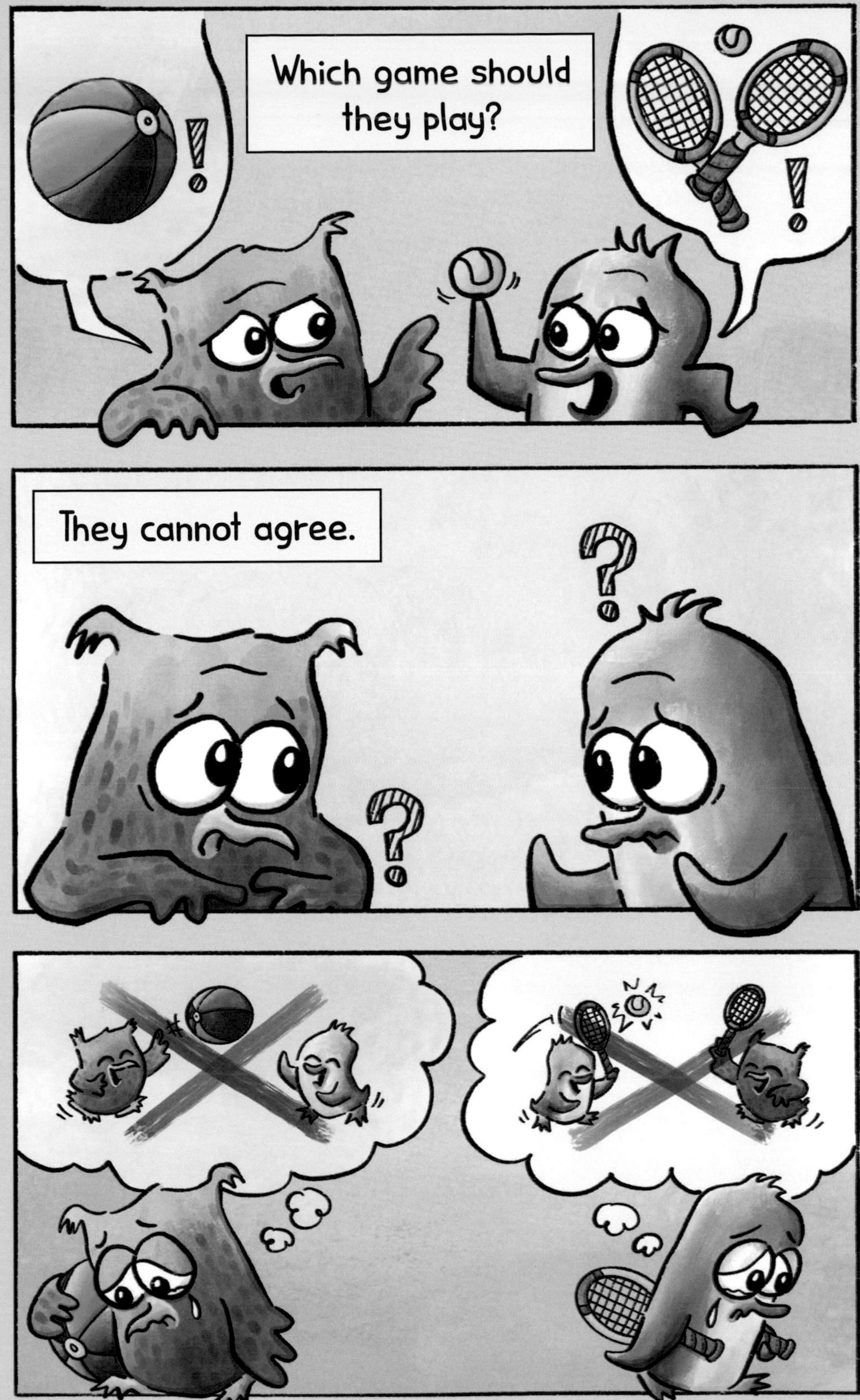
Which game should they play?
They cannot agree.

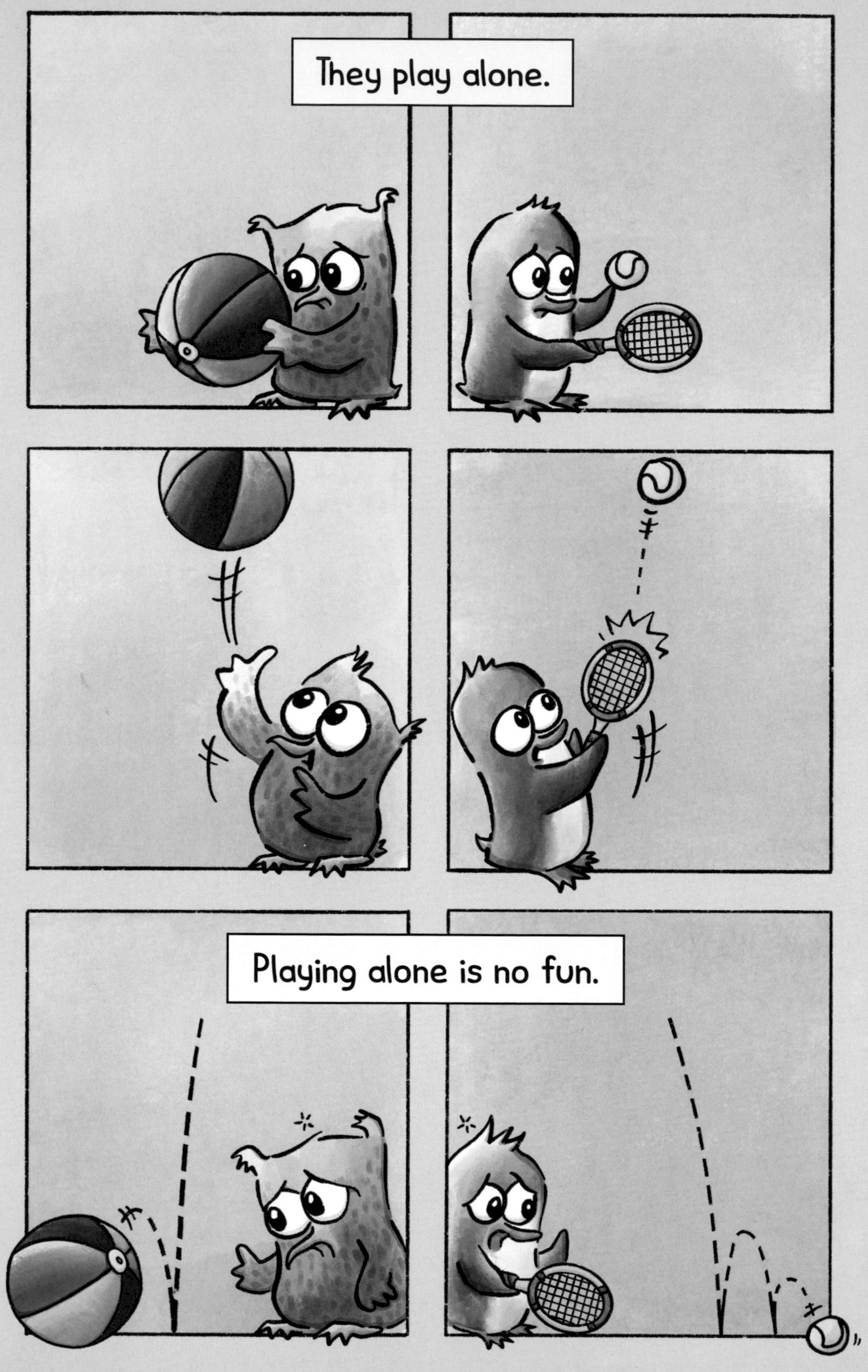
They play alone.
Playing alone is no fun.

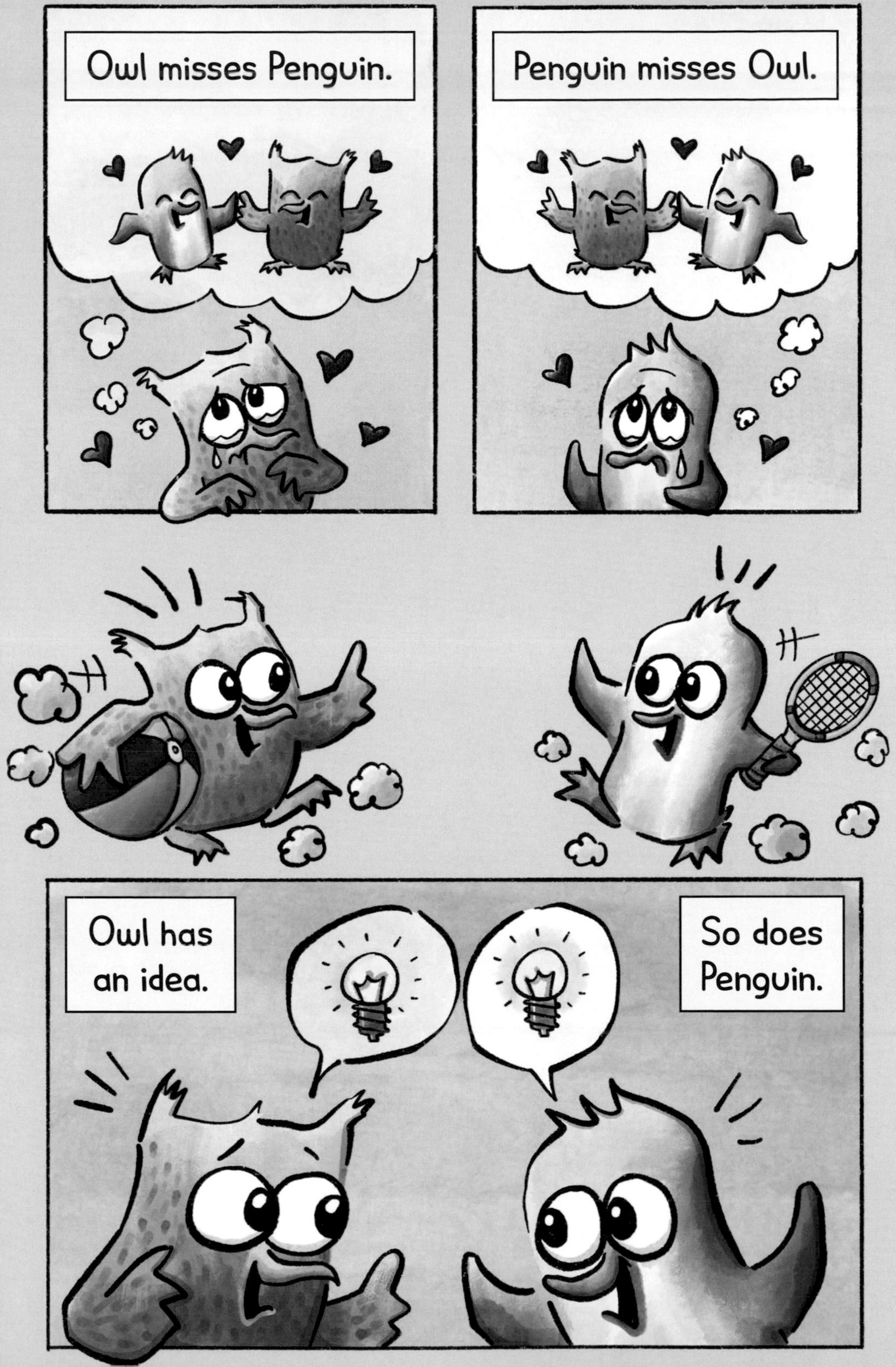
Owl misses Penguin.
Penguin misses Owl.
Owl has an idea.
So does Penguin.

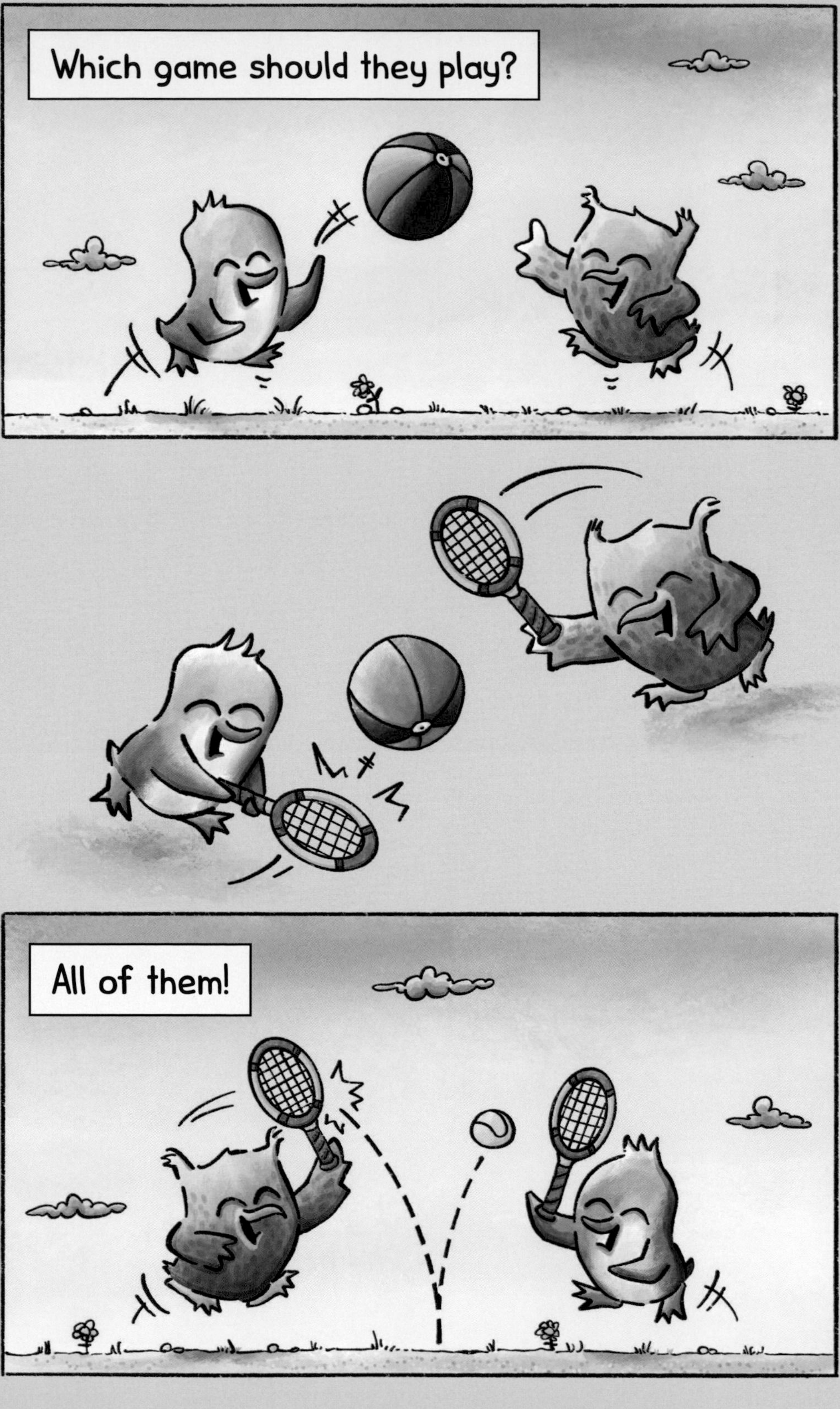
Which game should they play?
All of them!

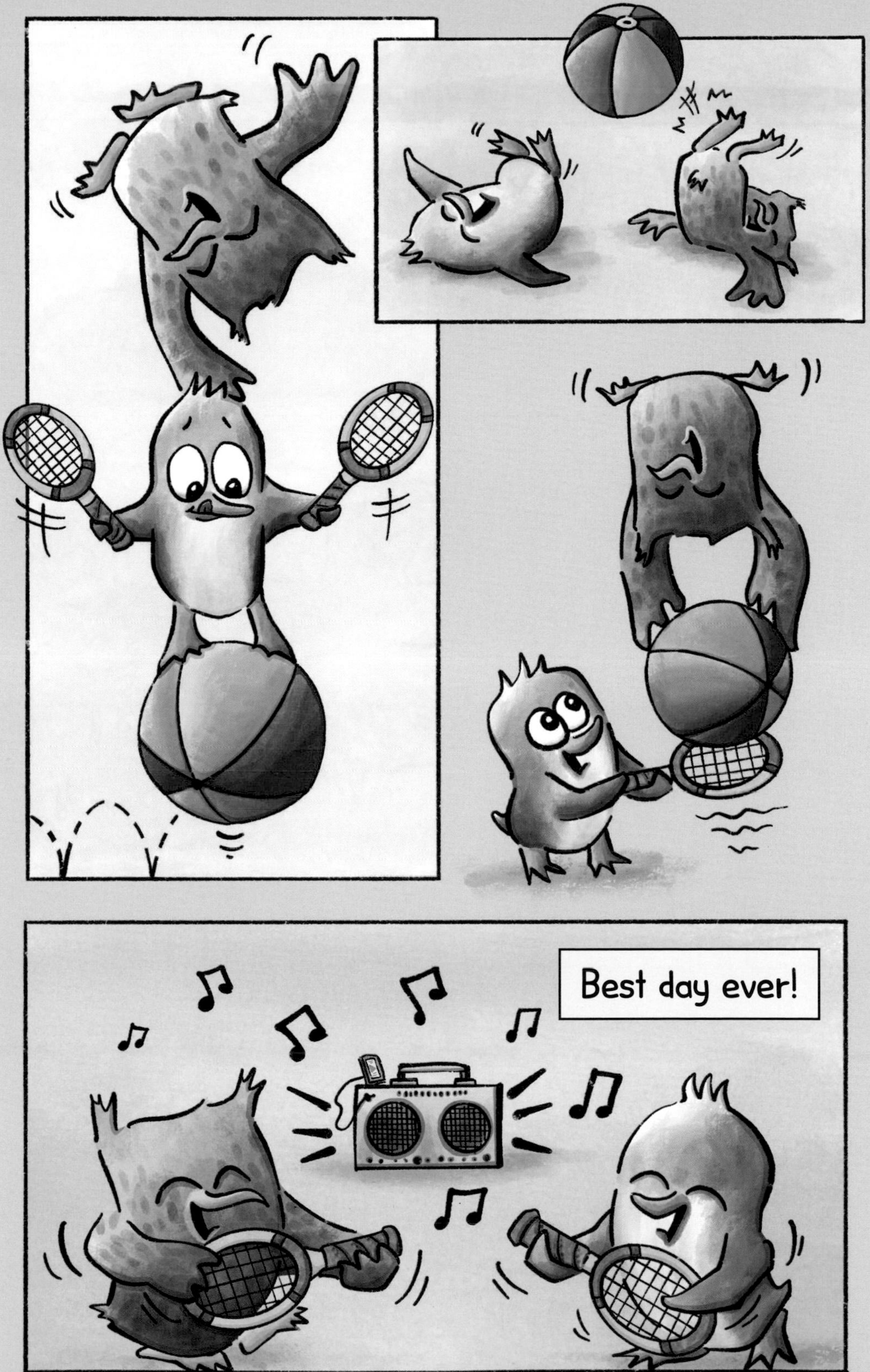
Best day ever!

END

FISH

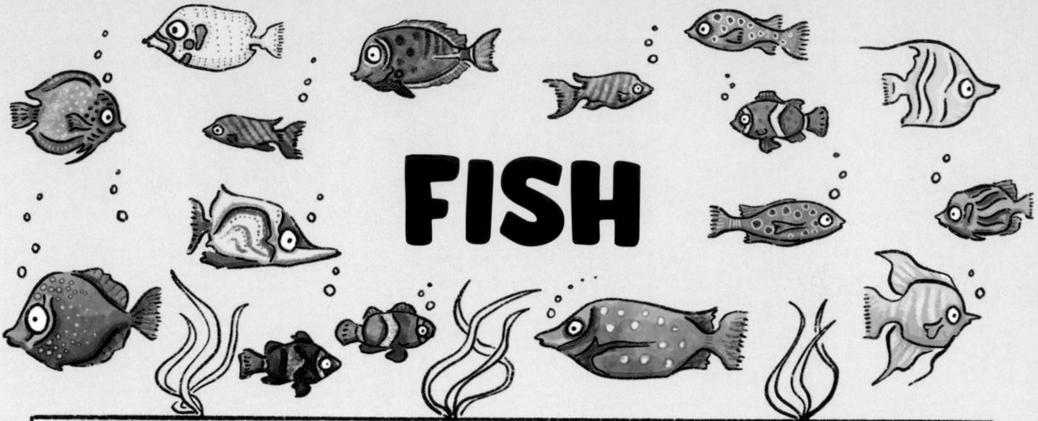

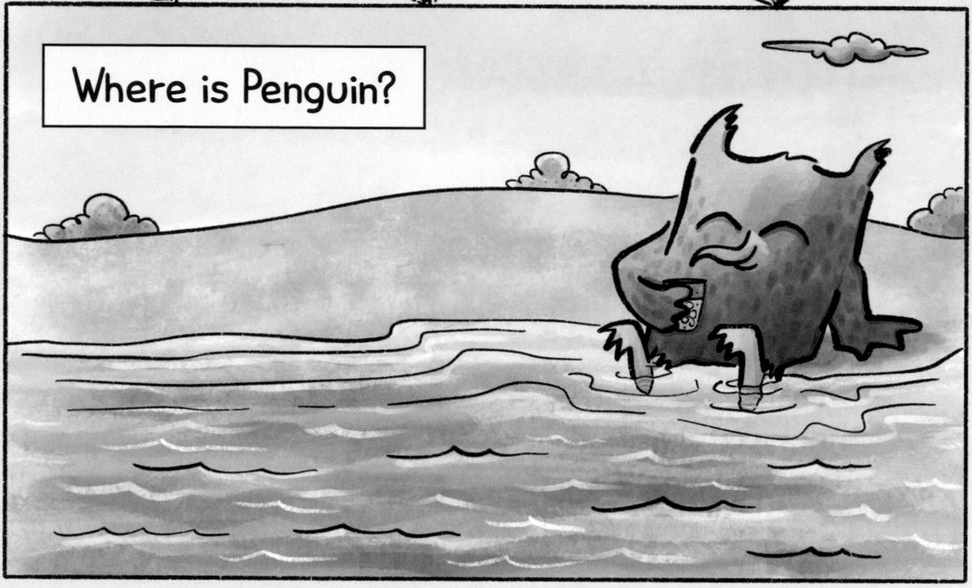
Where is Penguin?

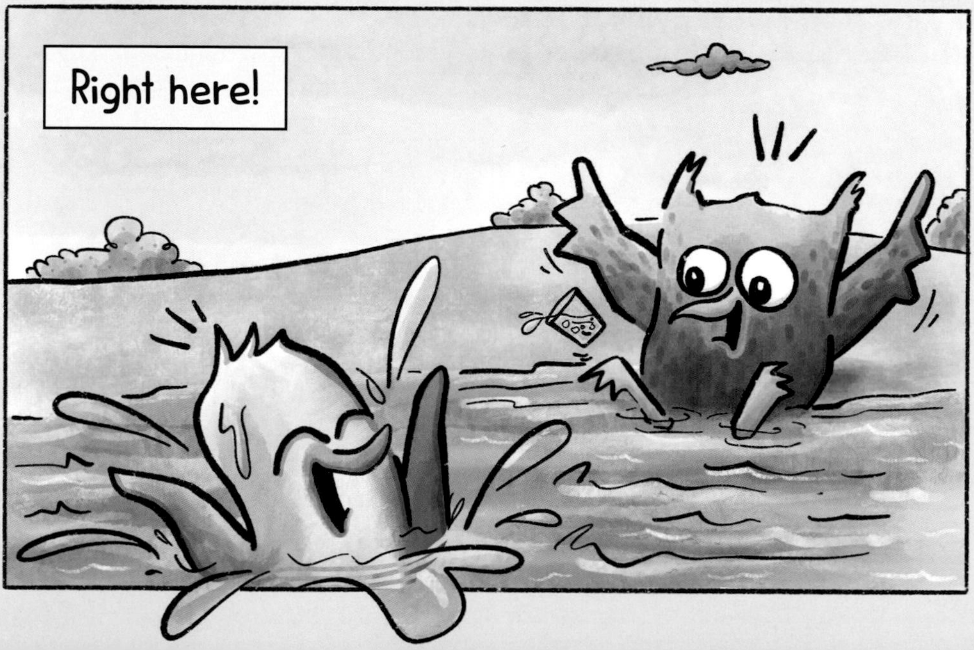
Right here!

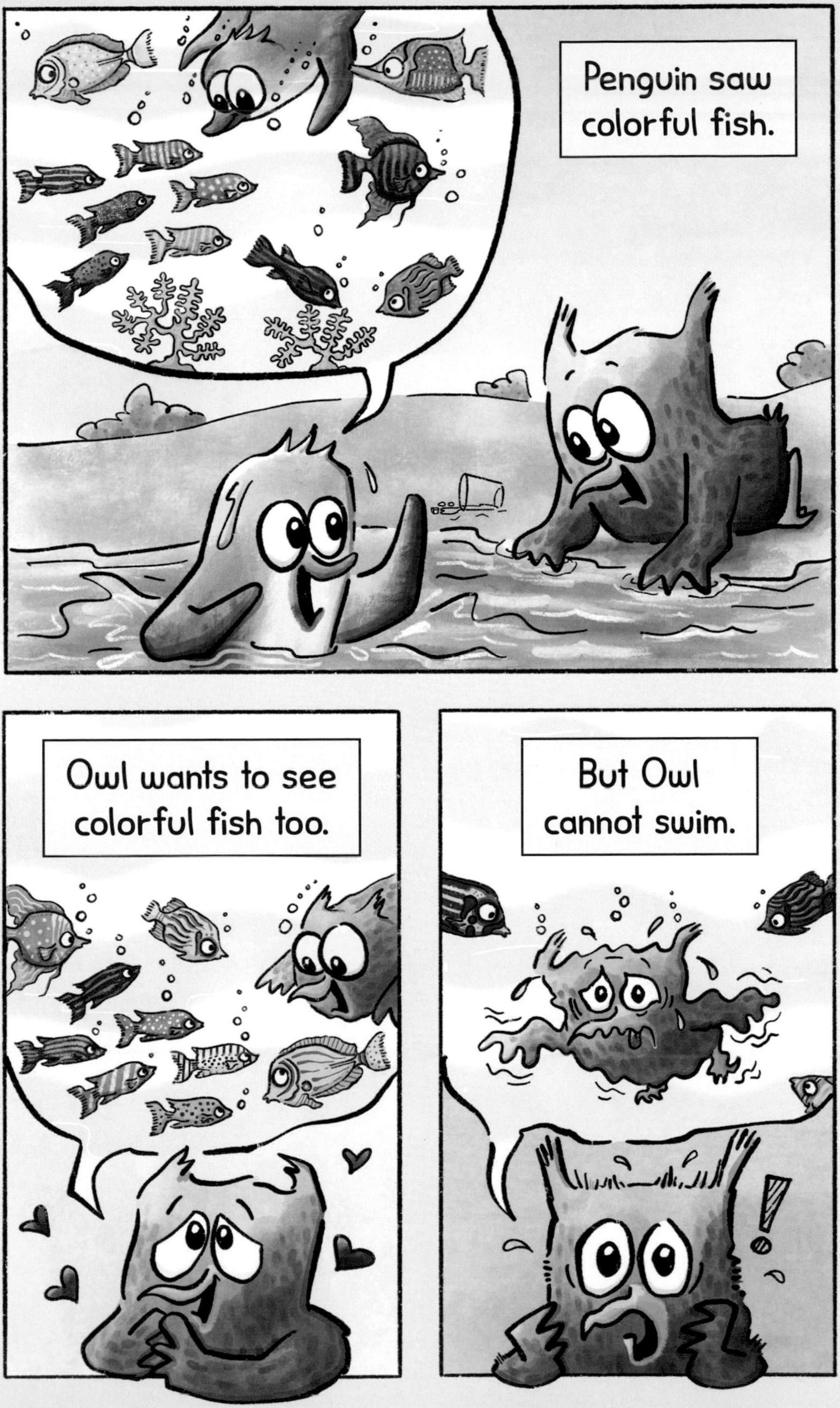
Penguin saw colorful fish.
Owl wants to see colorful fish too.
But Owl cannot swim.

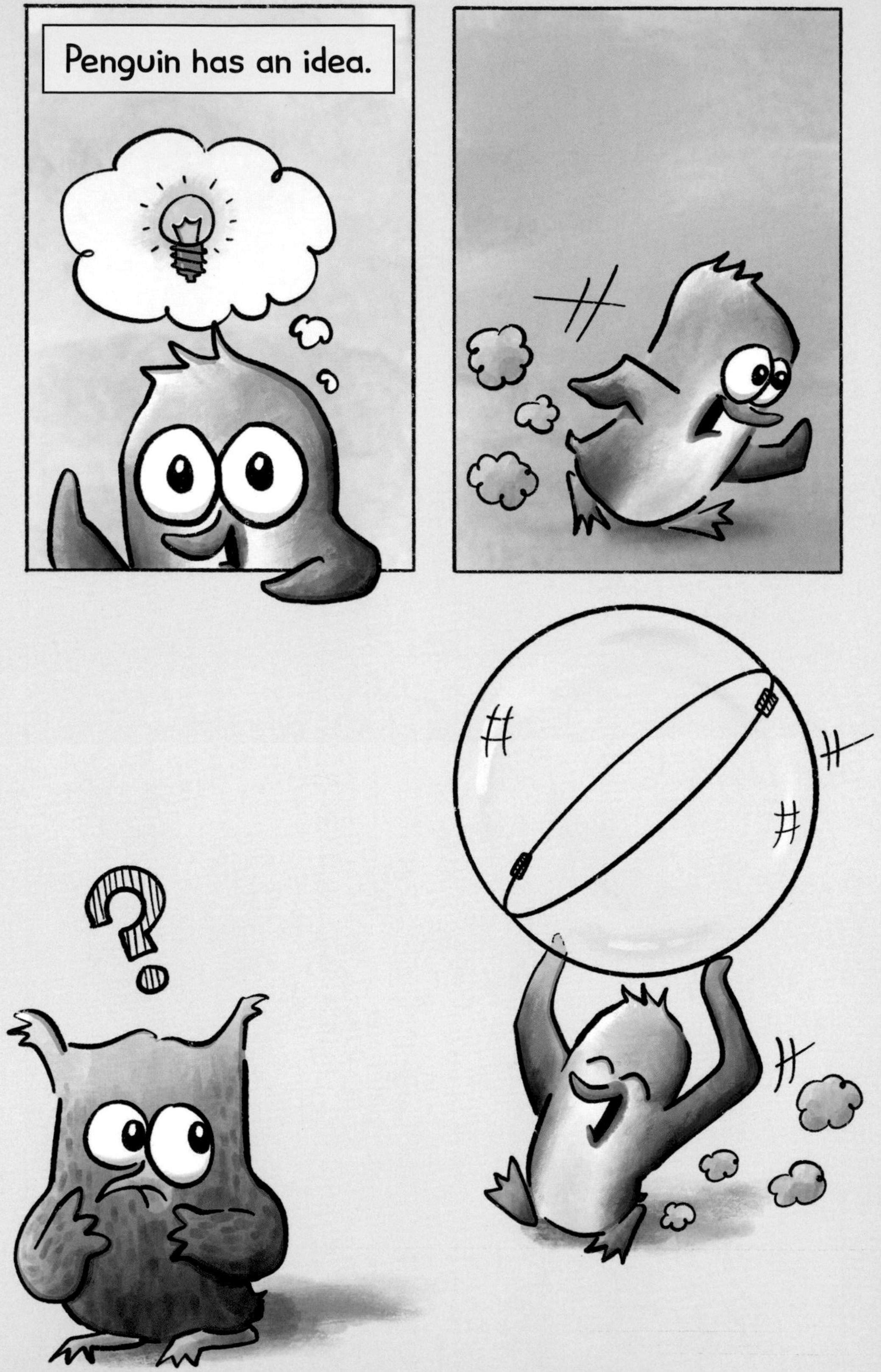
Penguin has an idea.

Owl can sit in the glass bowl and see the fish.

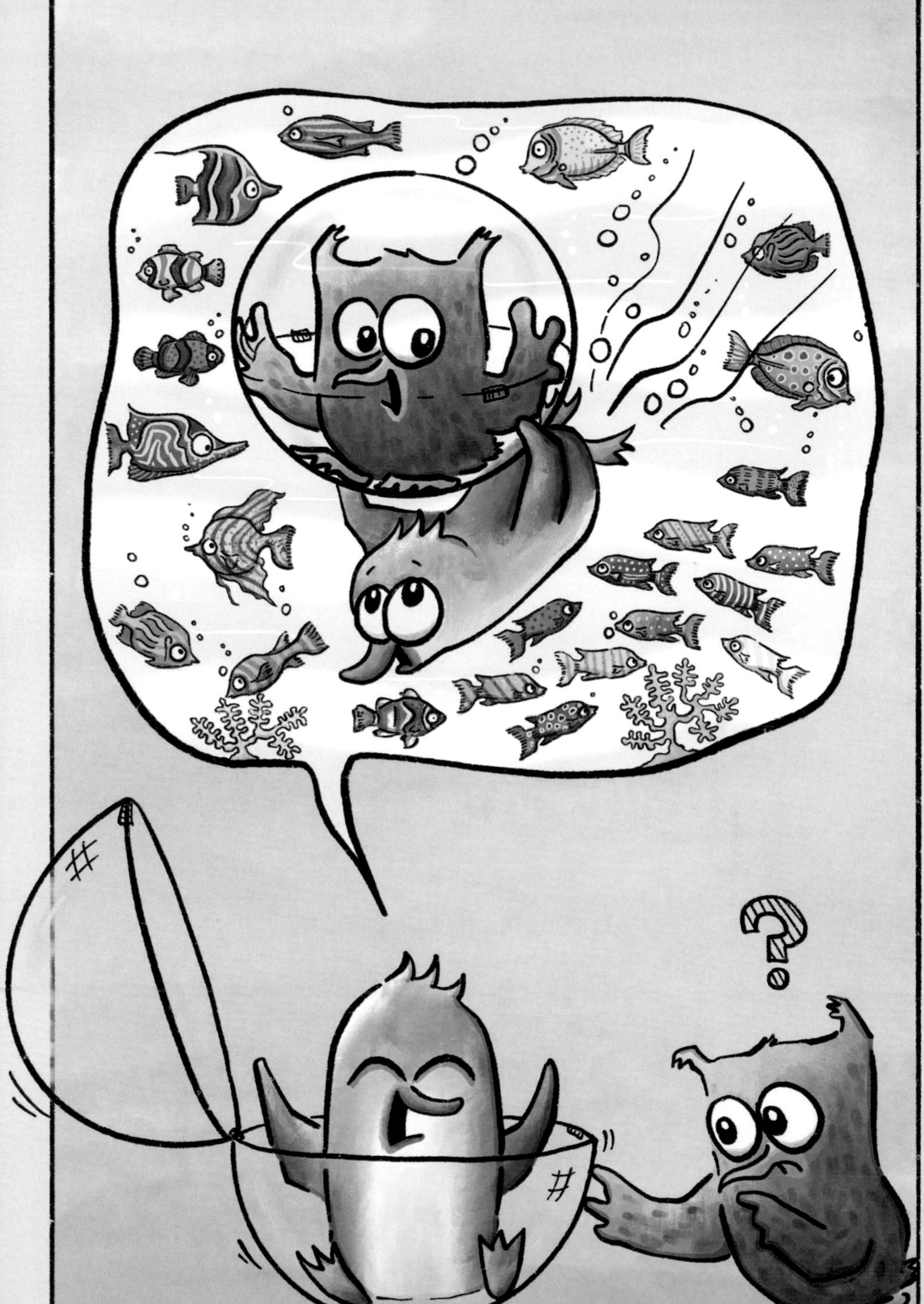

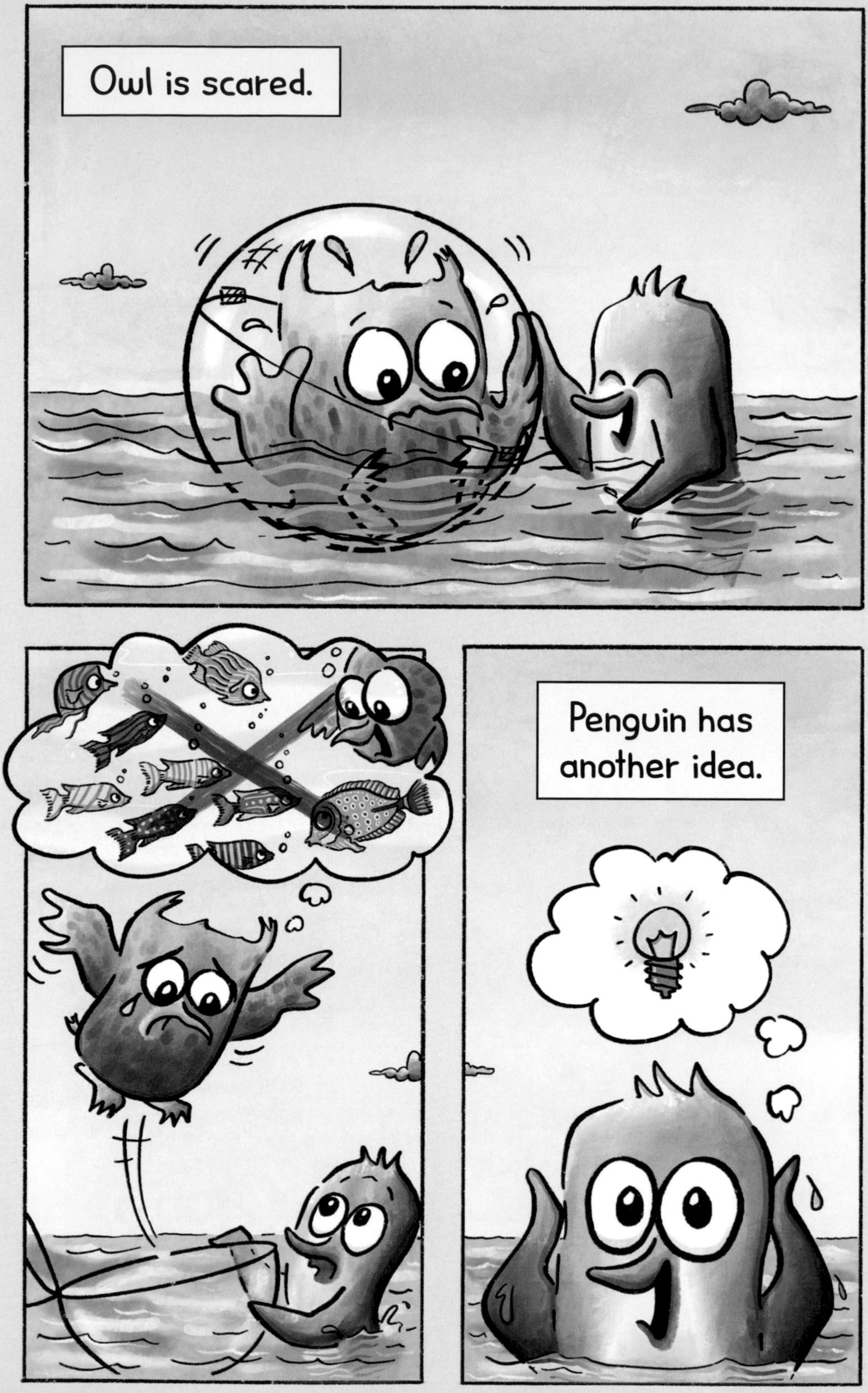
Owl is scared.
Penguin has another idea.

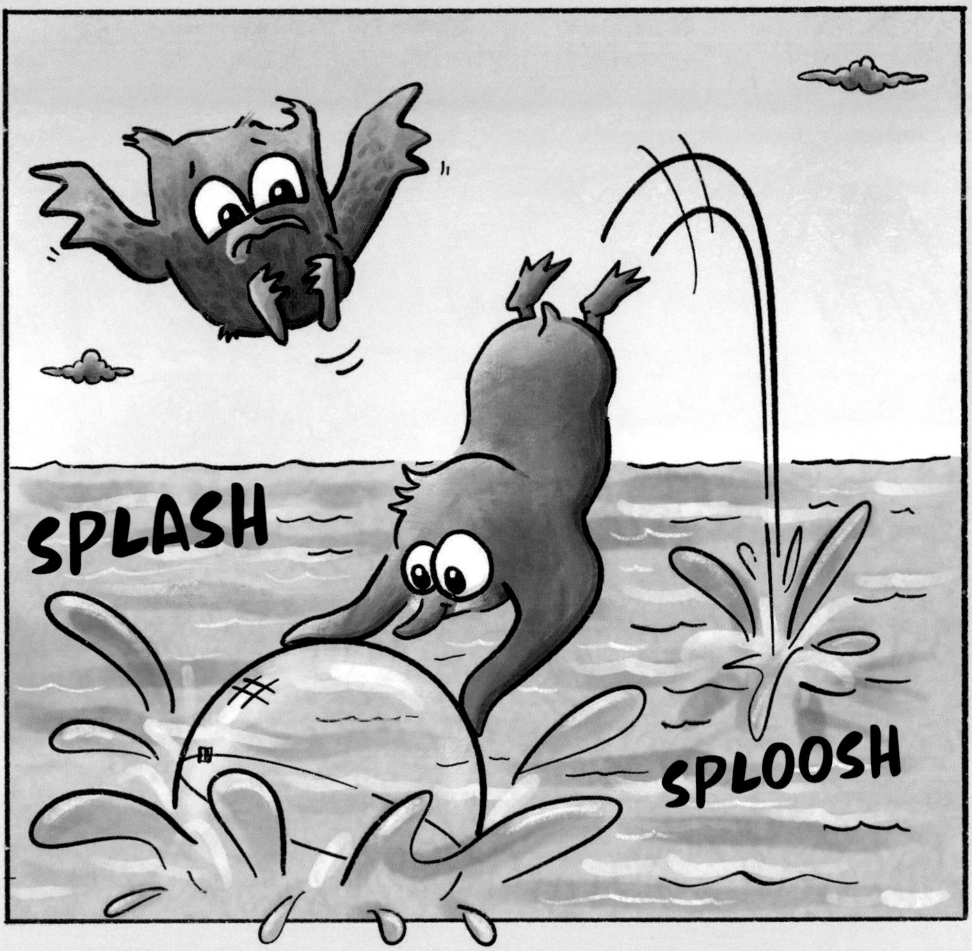
SPLASH
SPLOOSH

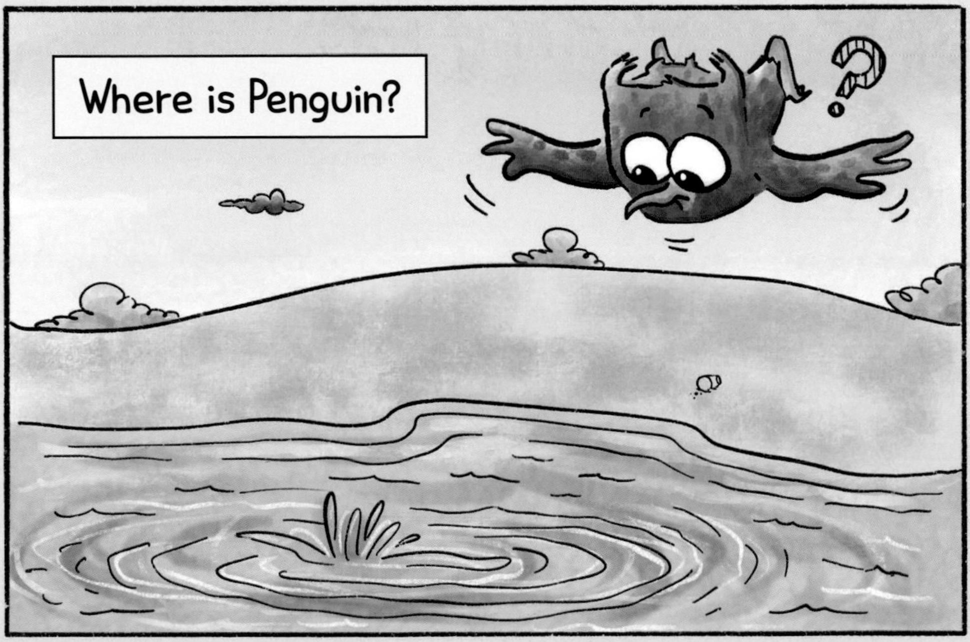
Where is Penguin?

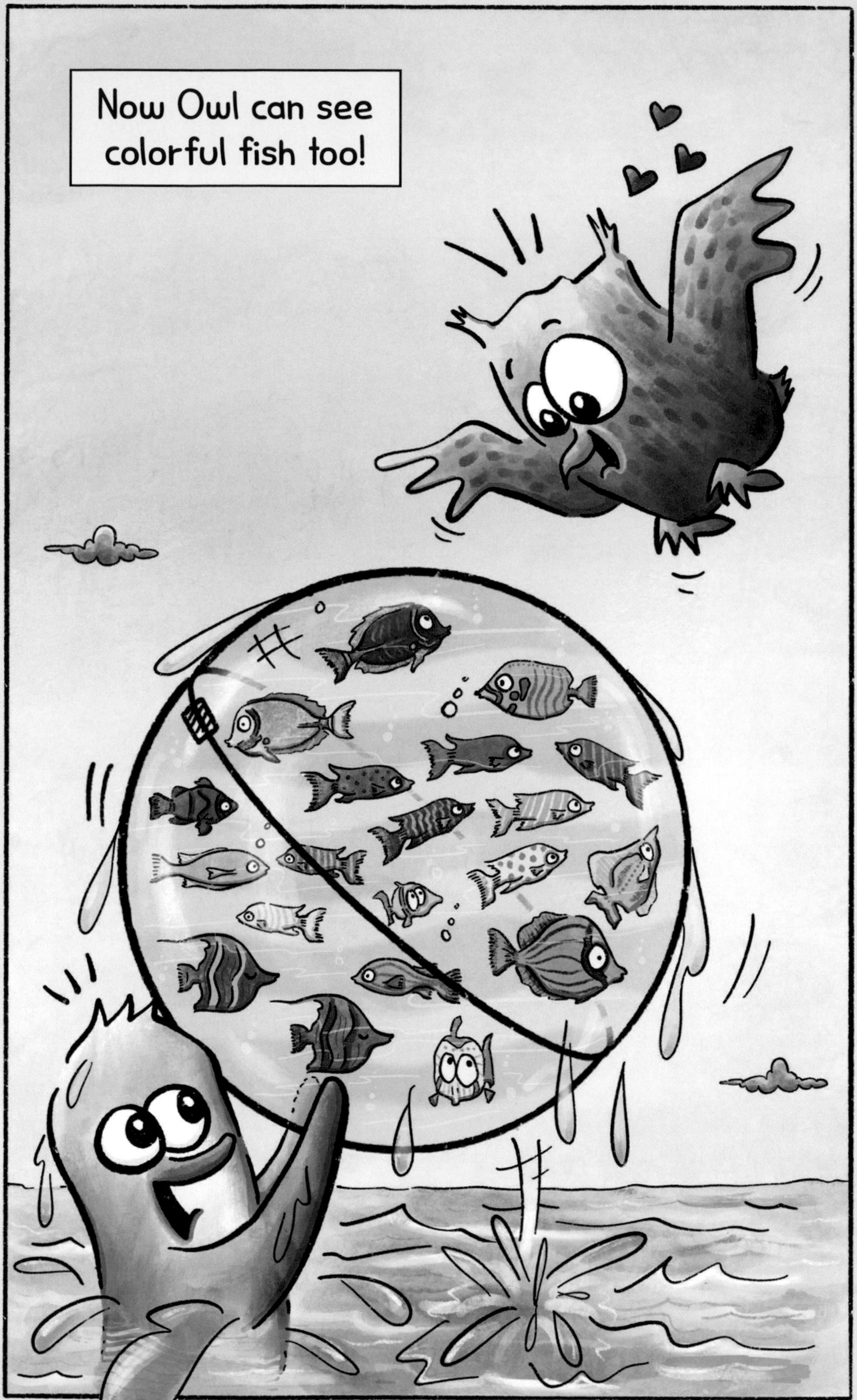
Now Owl can see
colorful fish too!

END

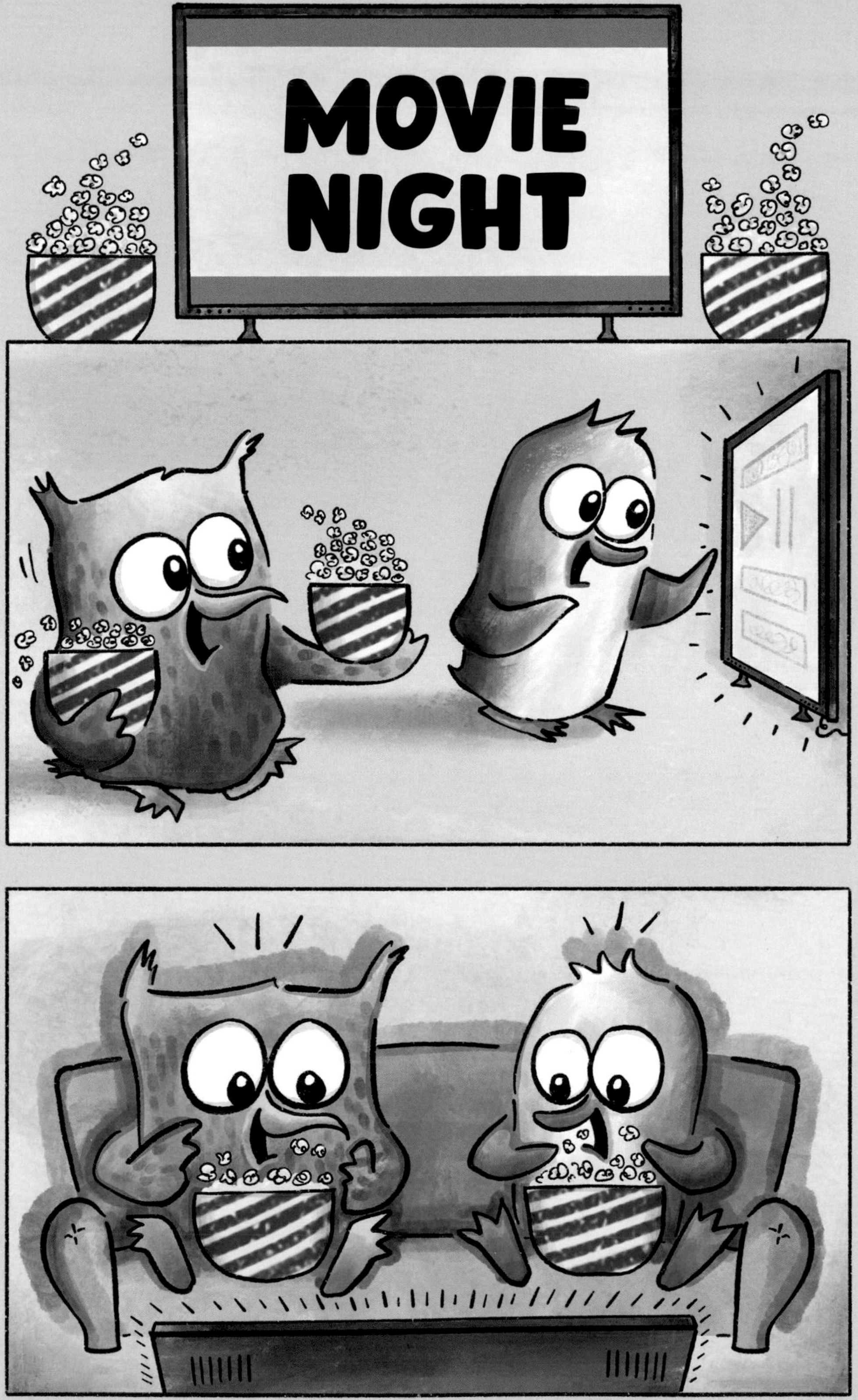
MOVIE NIGHT

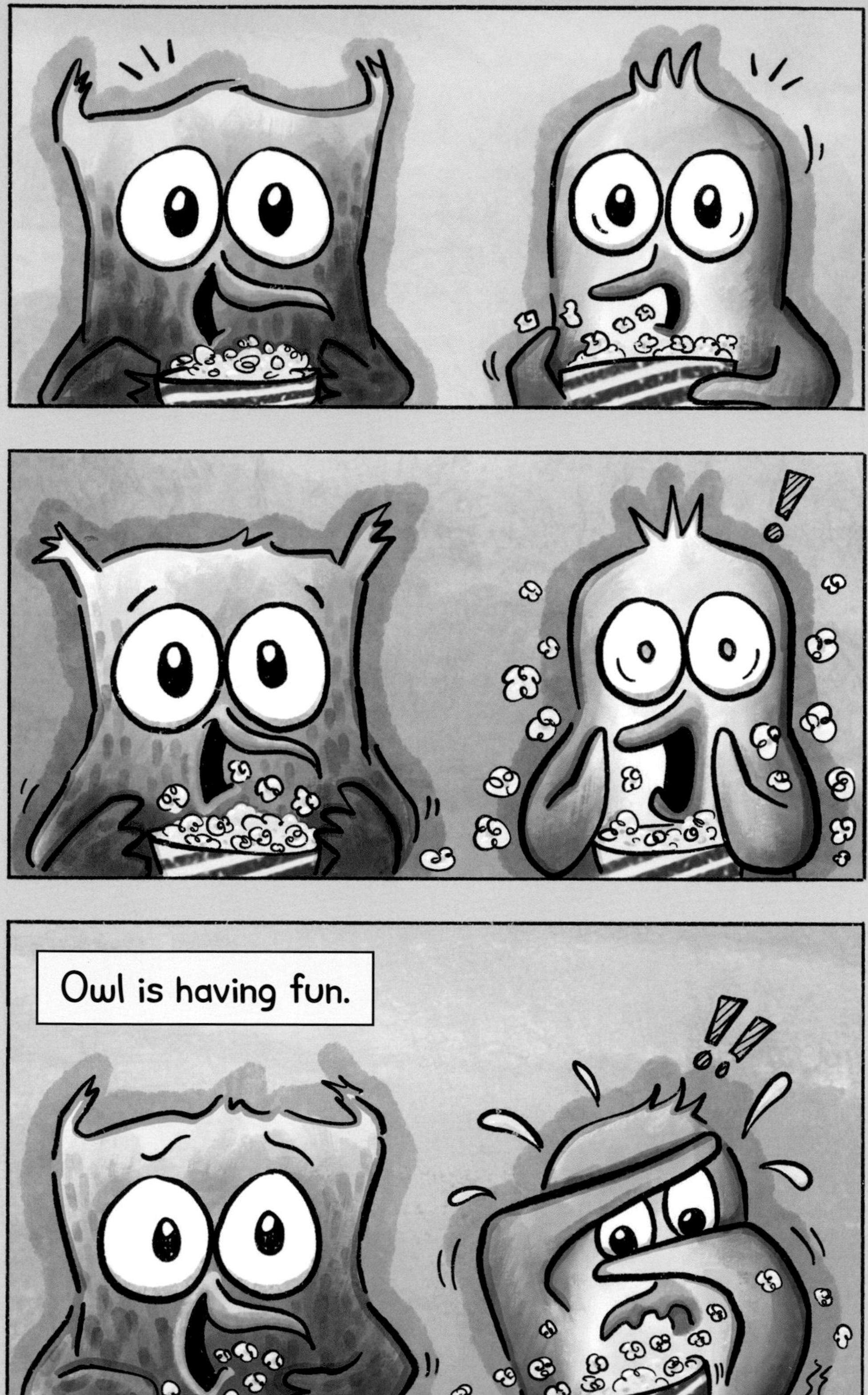
Owl is having fun.

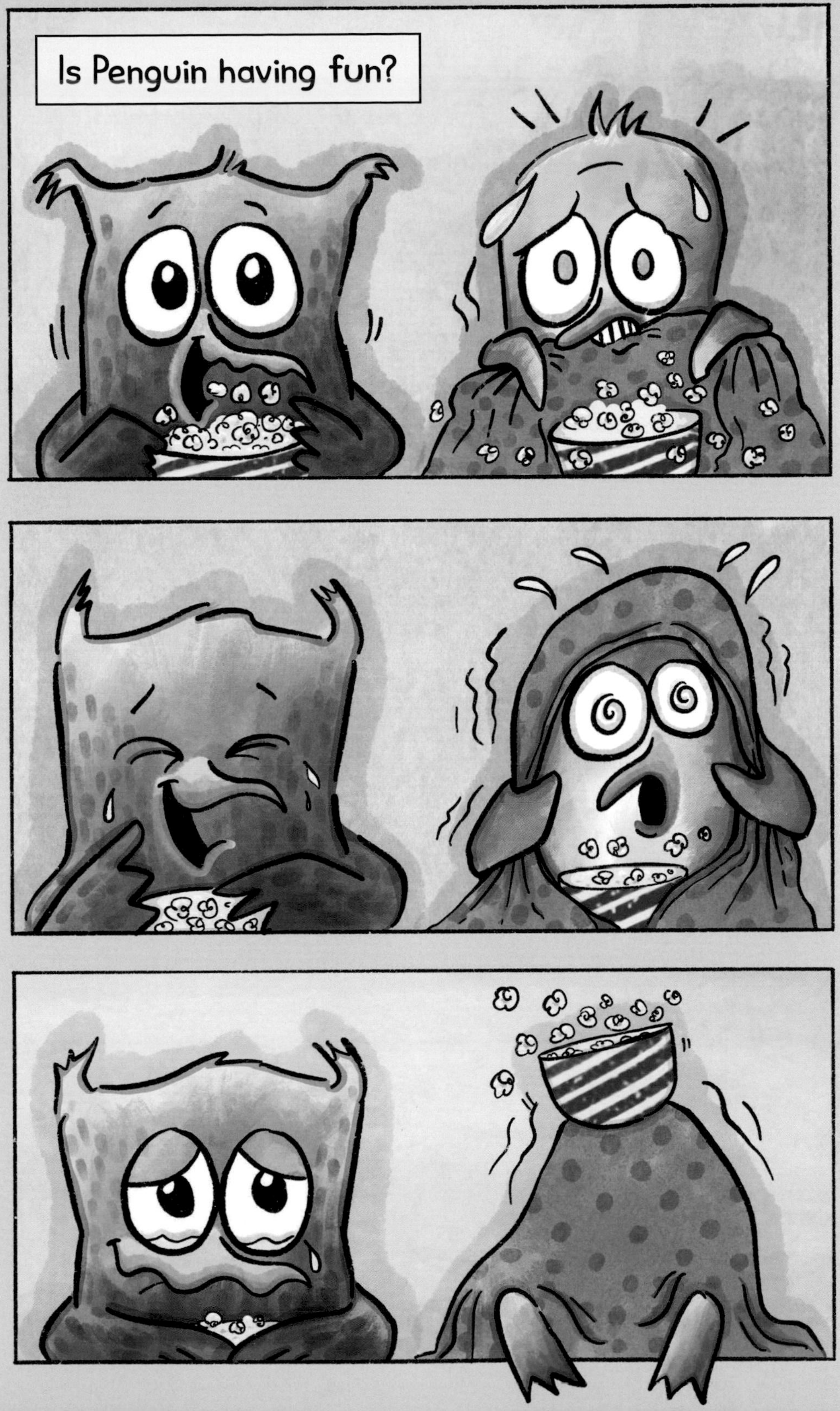
Is Penguin having fun?

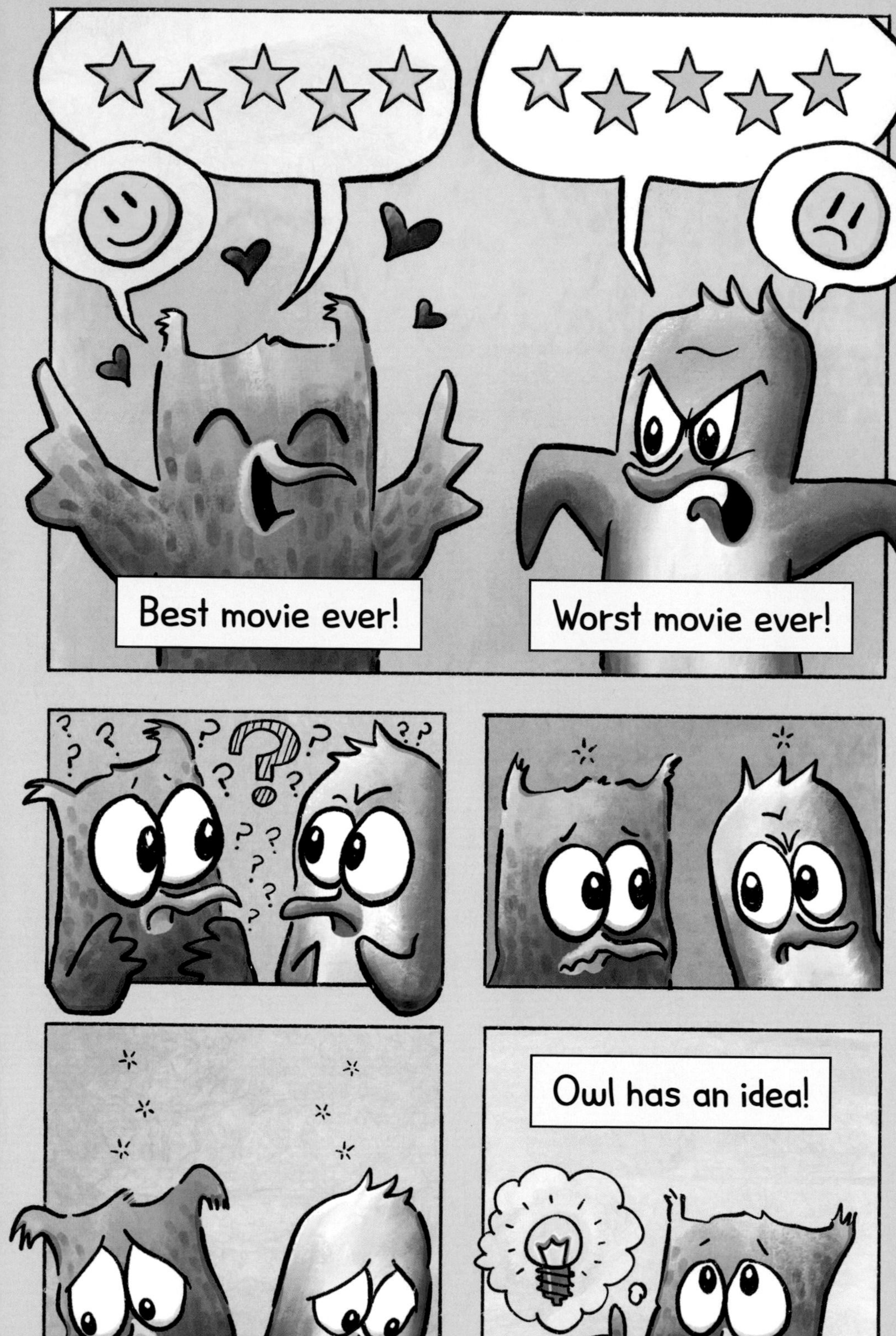
Best movie ever!
Worst movie ever!
Owl has an idea!

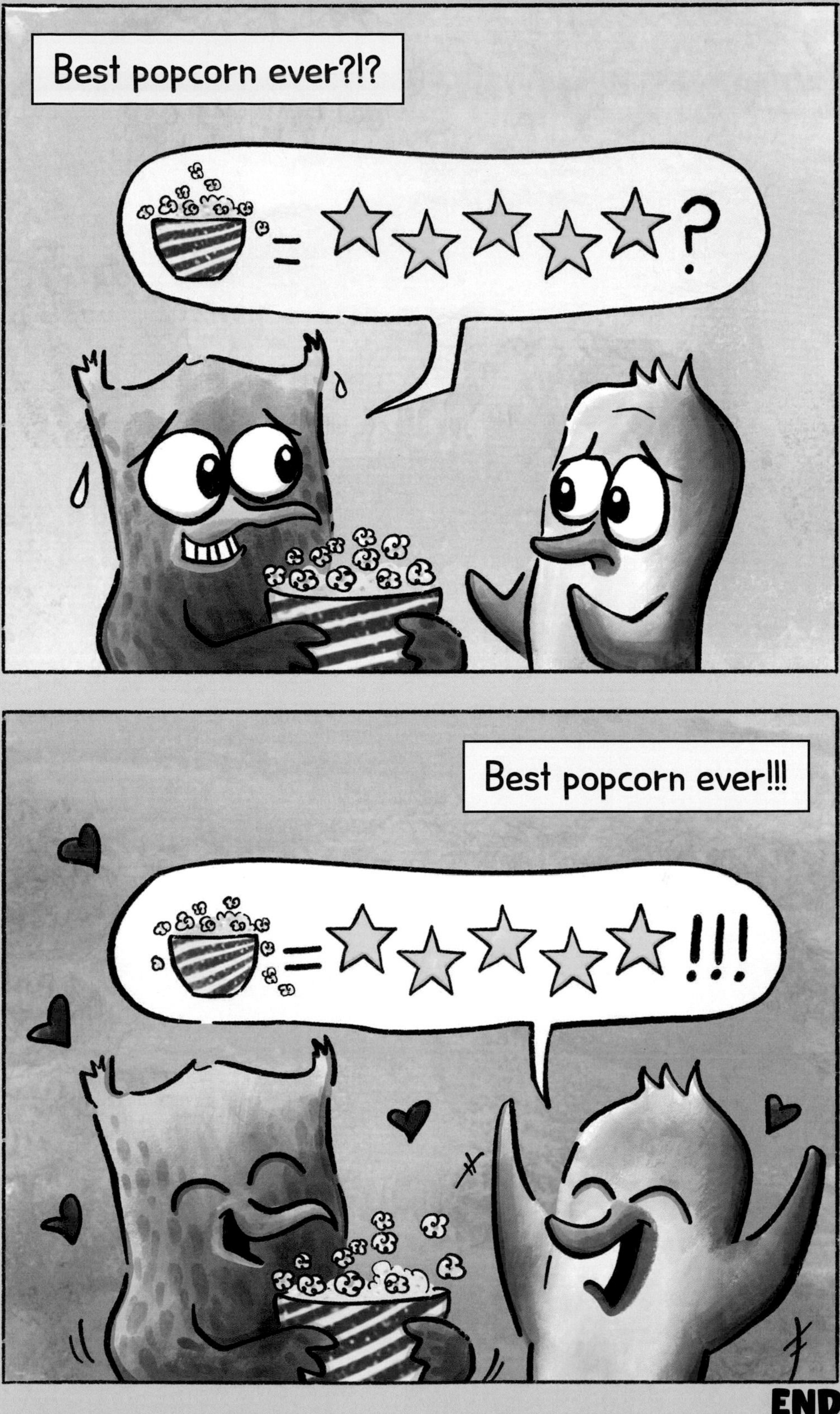
Best popcorn ever?!?
=?
Best popcorn ever!!!
=!!!

END

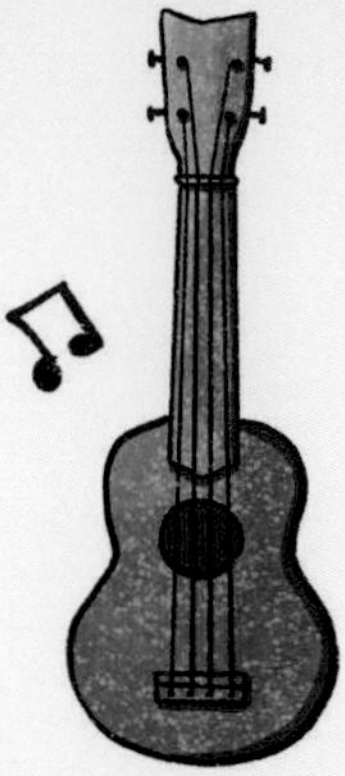

MAKING MUSIC

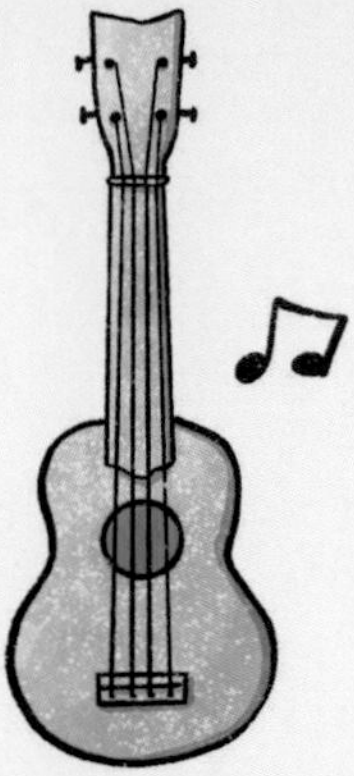

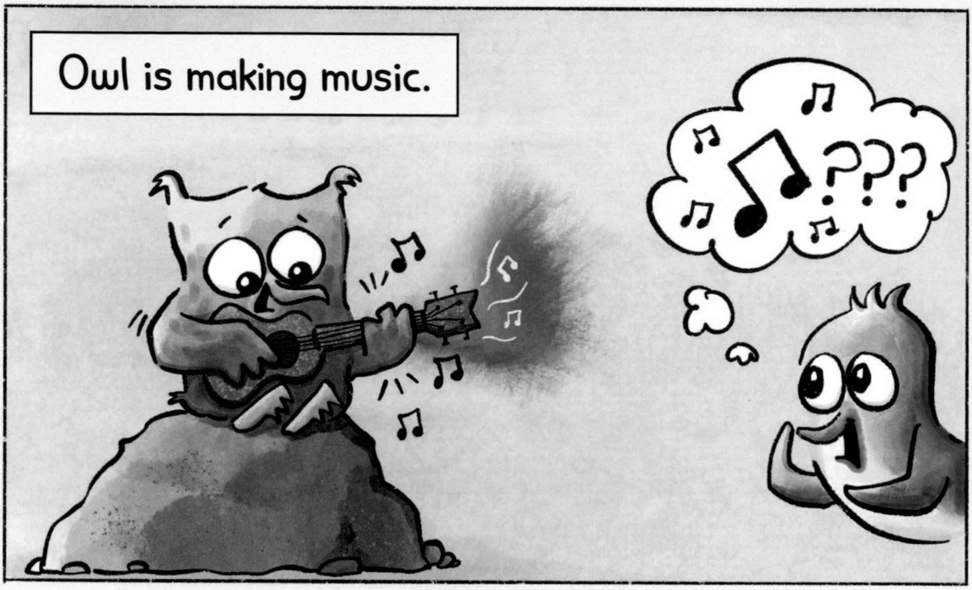
Owl is making music.
???

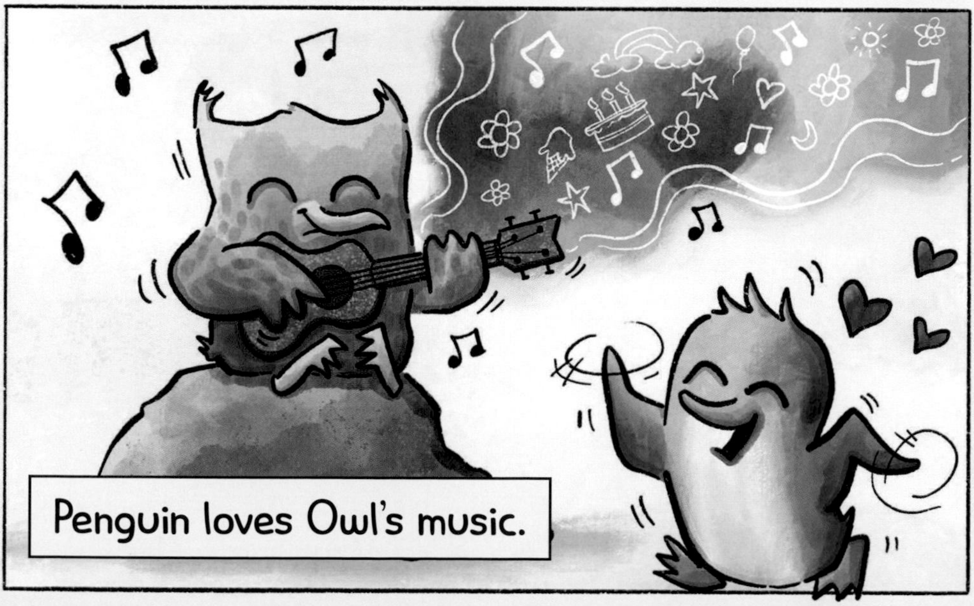
Penguin loves Owl's music.

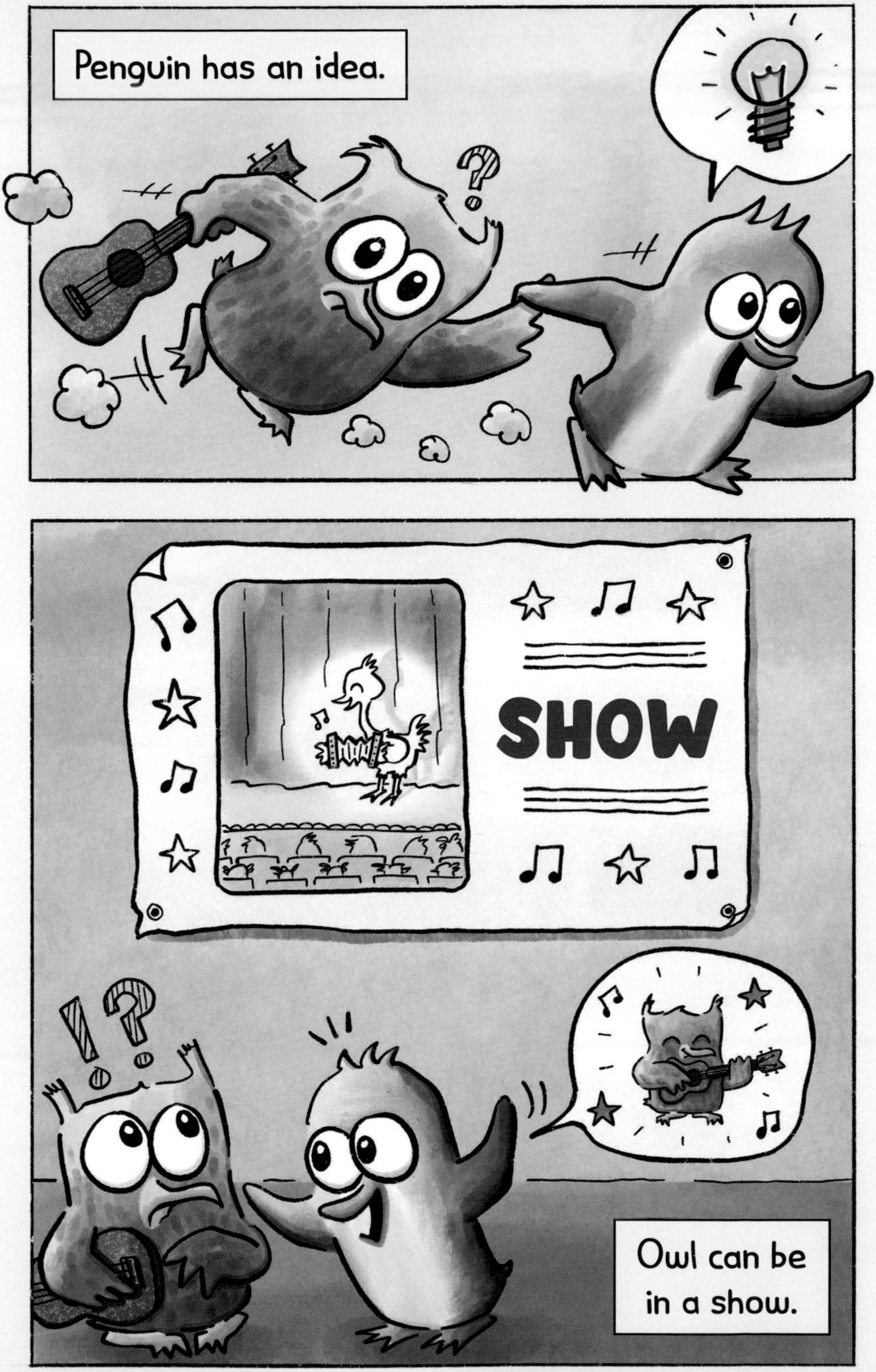
Penguin has an idea.
SHOW
Owl can be in a show.

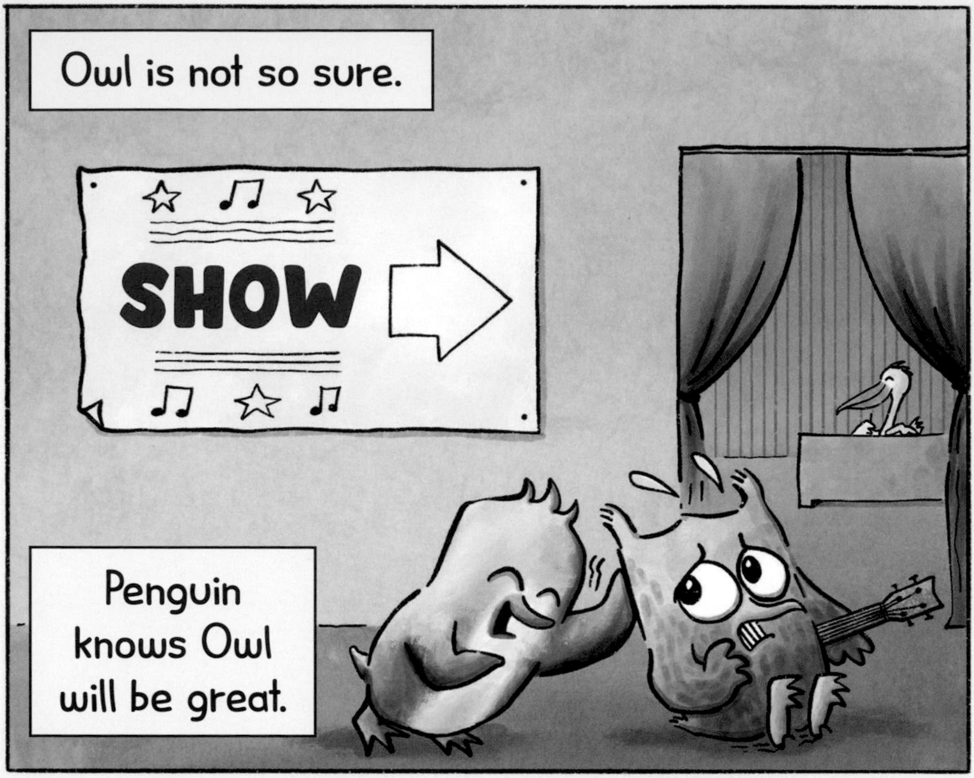
Owl is not so sure.
SHOW
Penguin knows Owl will be great.

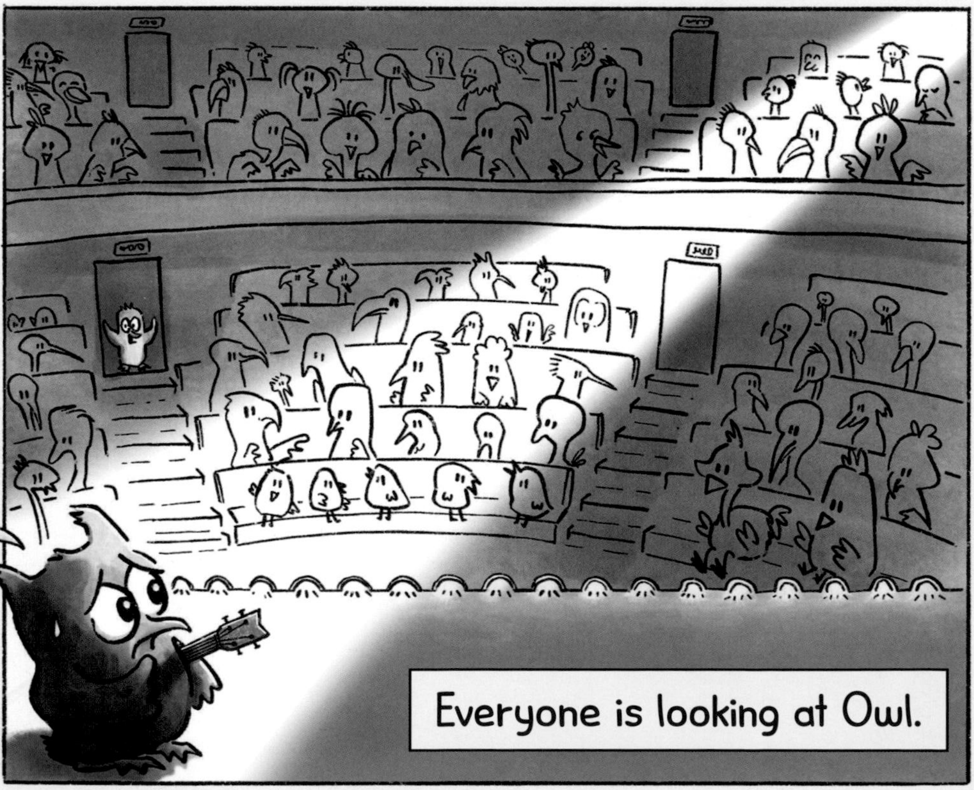
Everyone is looking at Owl.

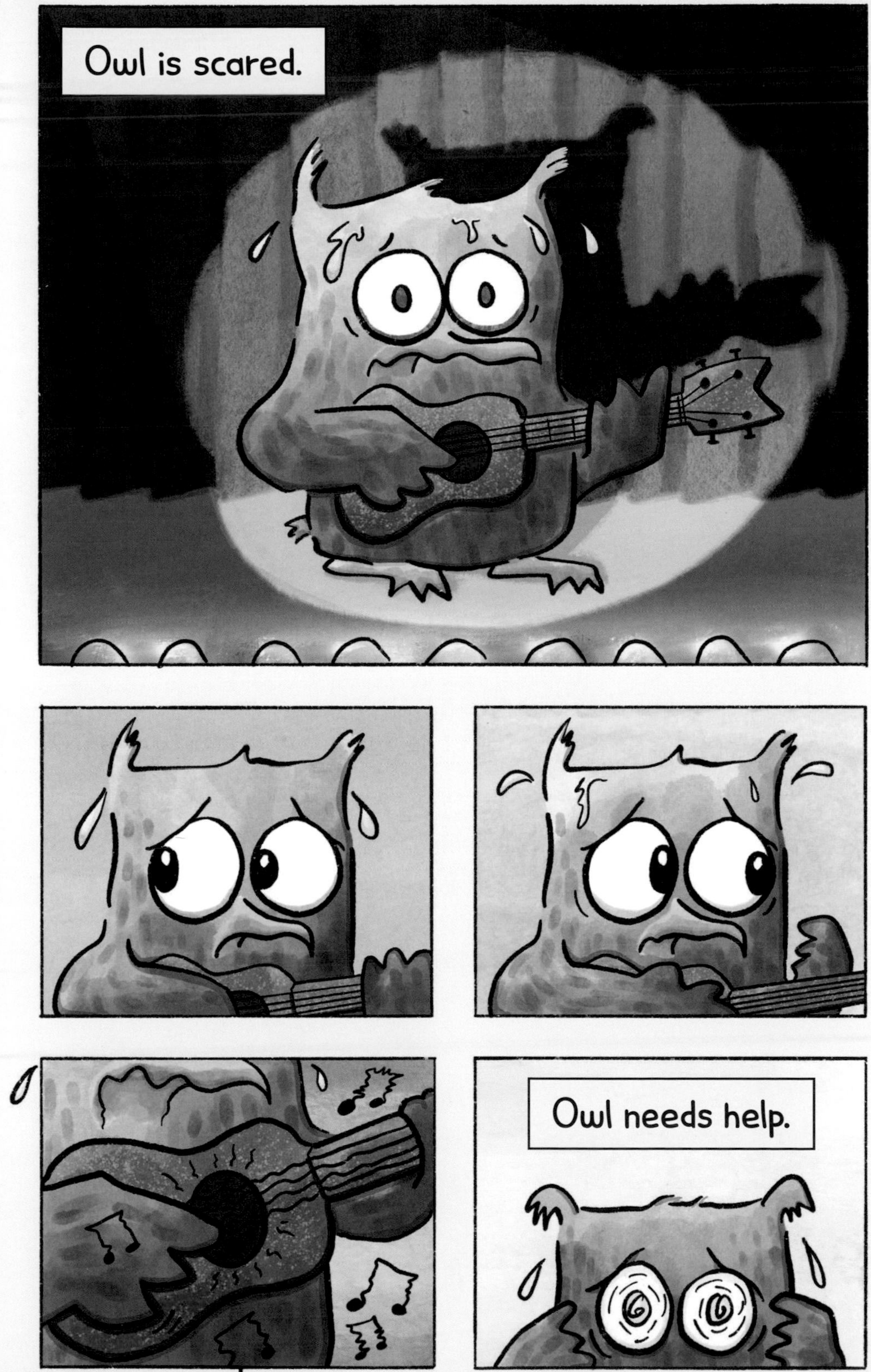
Owl is scared.
Owl needs help.

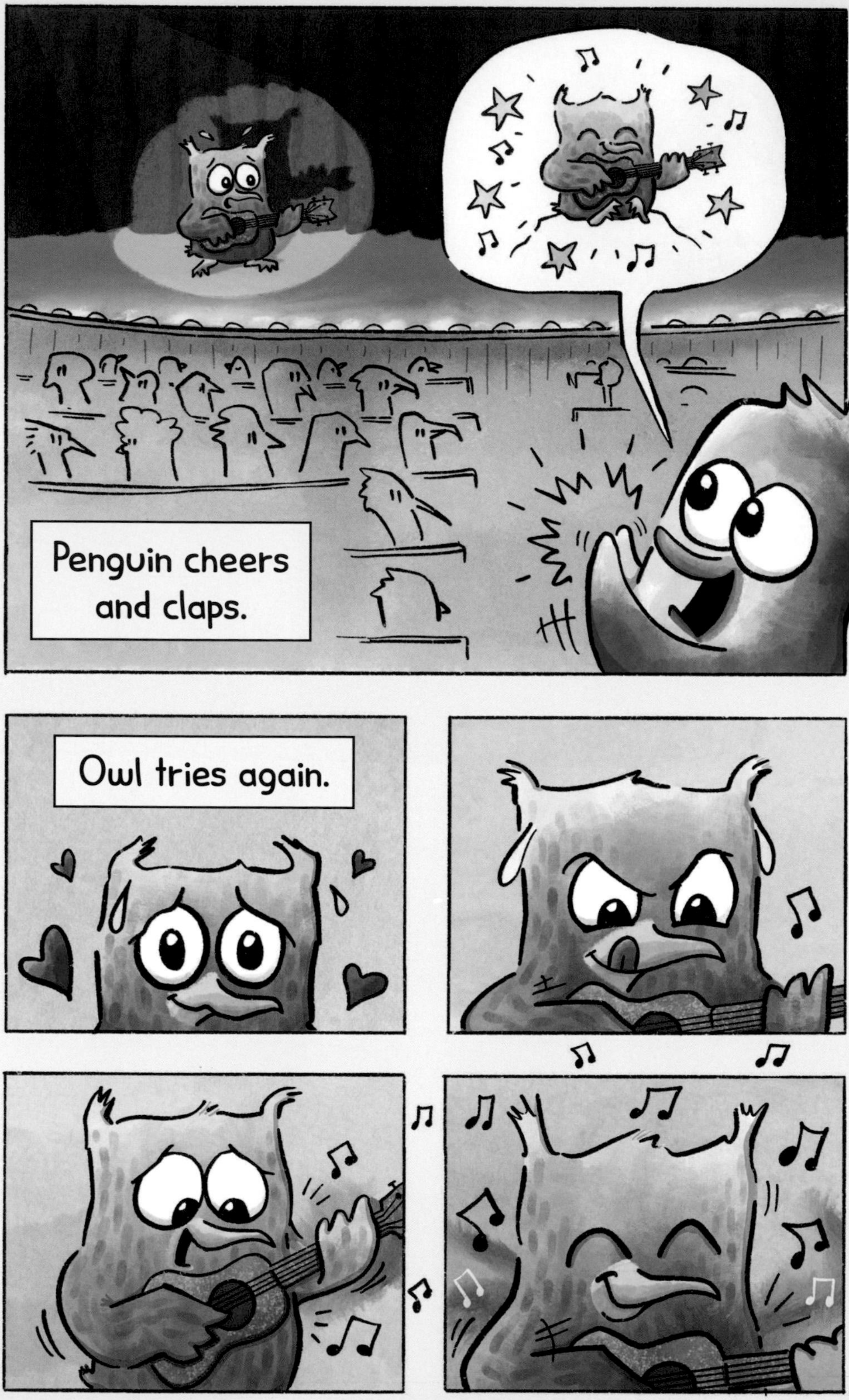
Penguin cheers and claps.
Owl tries again.

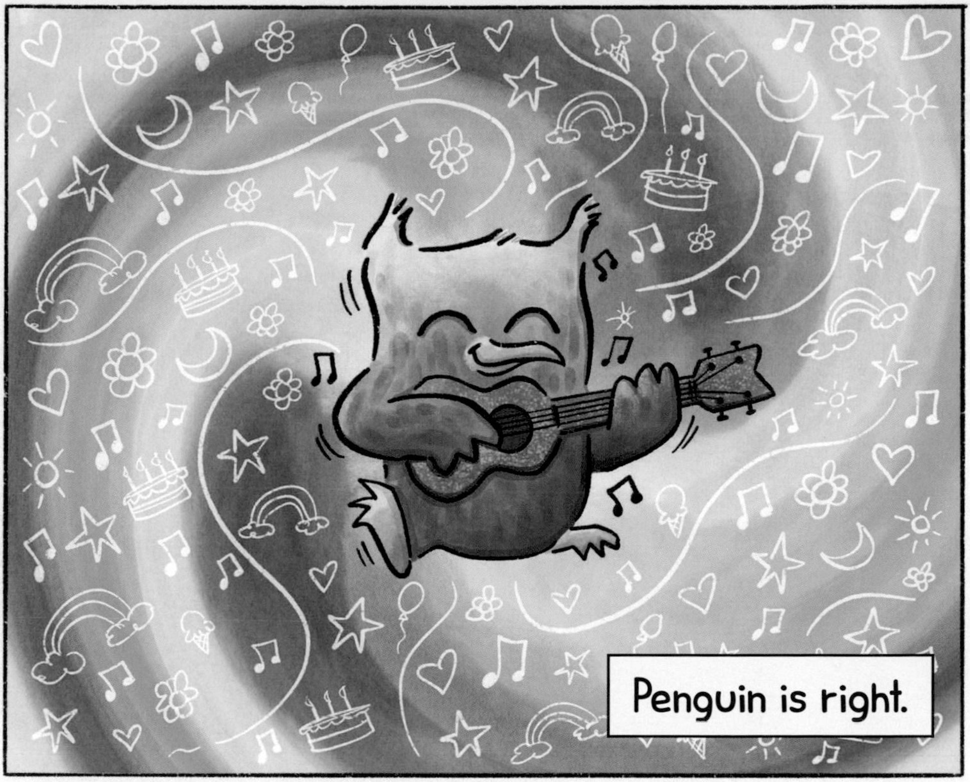
Penguin is right.

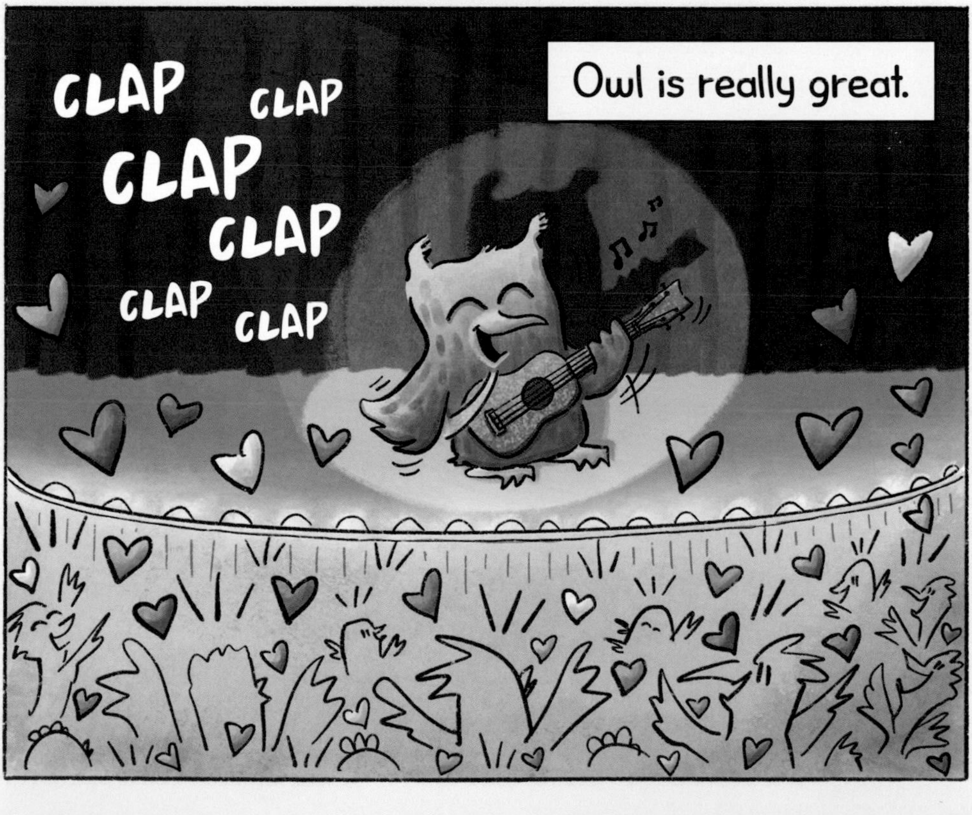
Owl is really great.
CLAP
CLAP
CLAP
CLAP
CLAP
CLAP

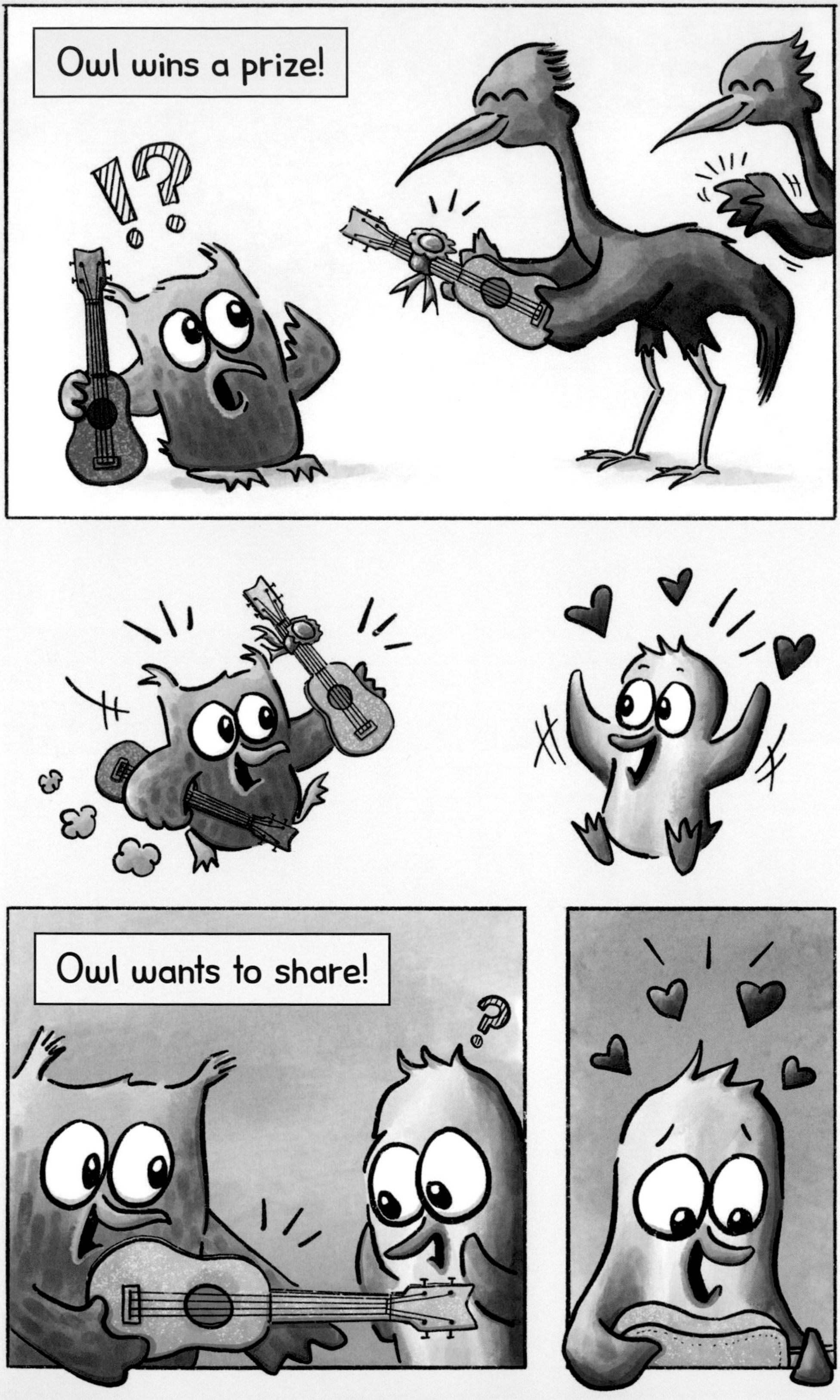
Owl wins a prize!
Owl wants to share!

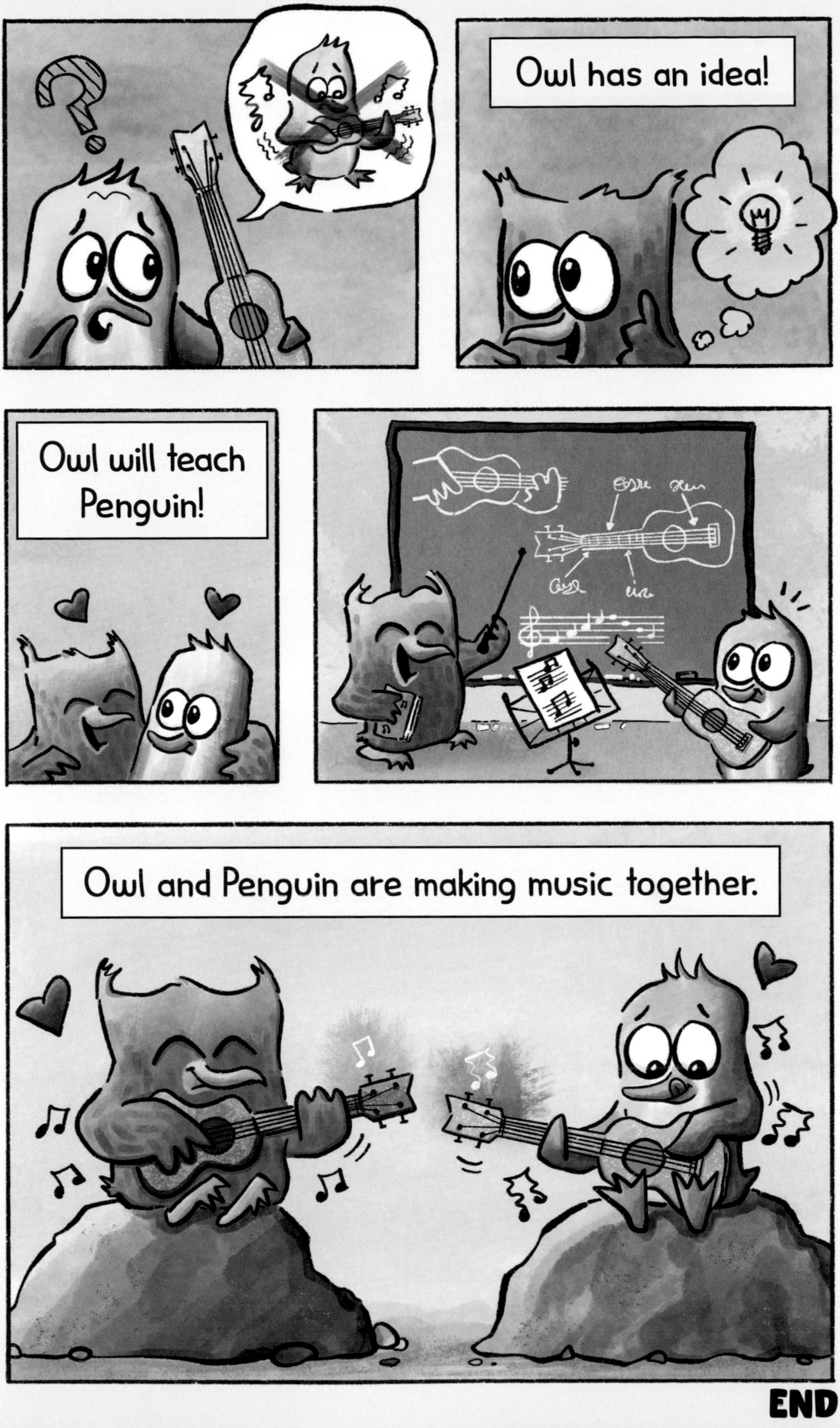
Owl has an idea!
Owl will teach Penguin!
Owl and Penguin are making music together.
END

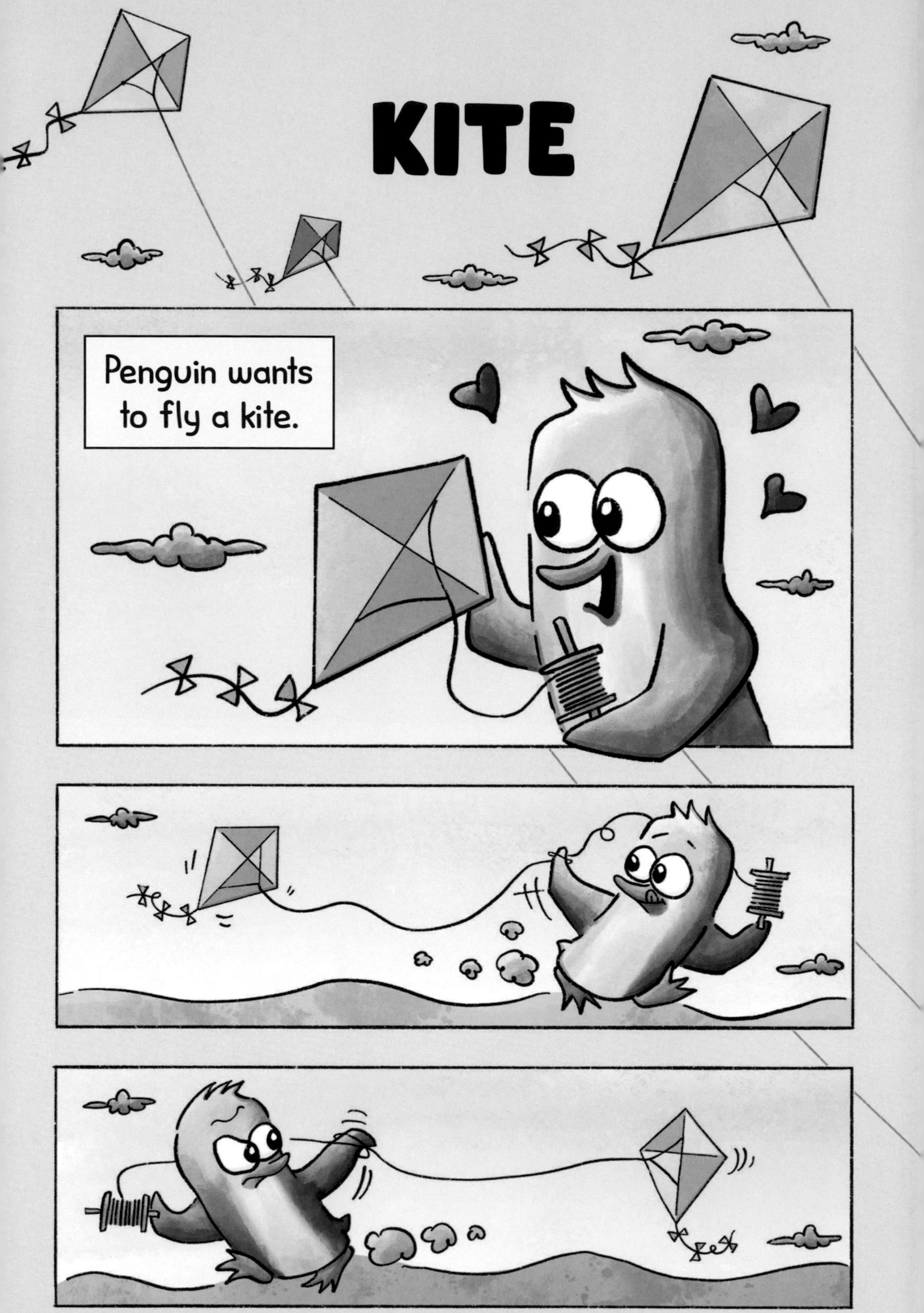
KITE
Penguin wants to fly a kite.

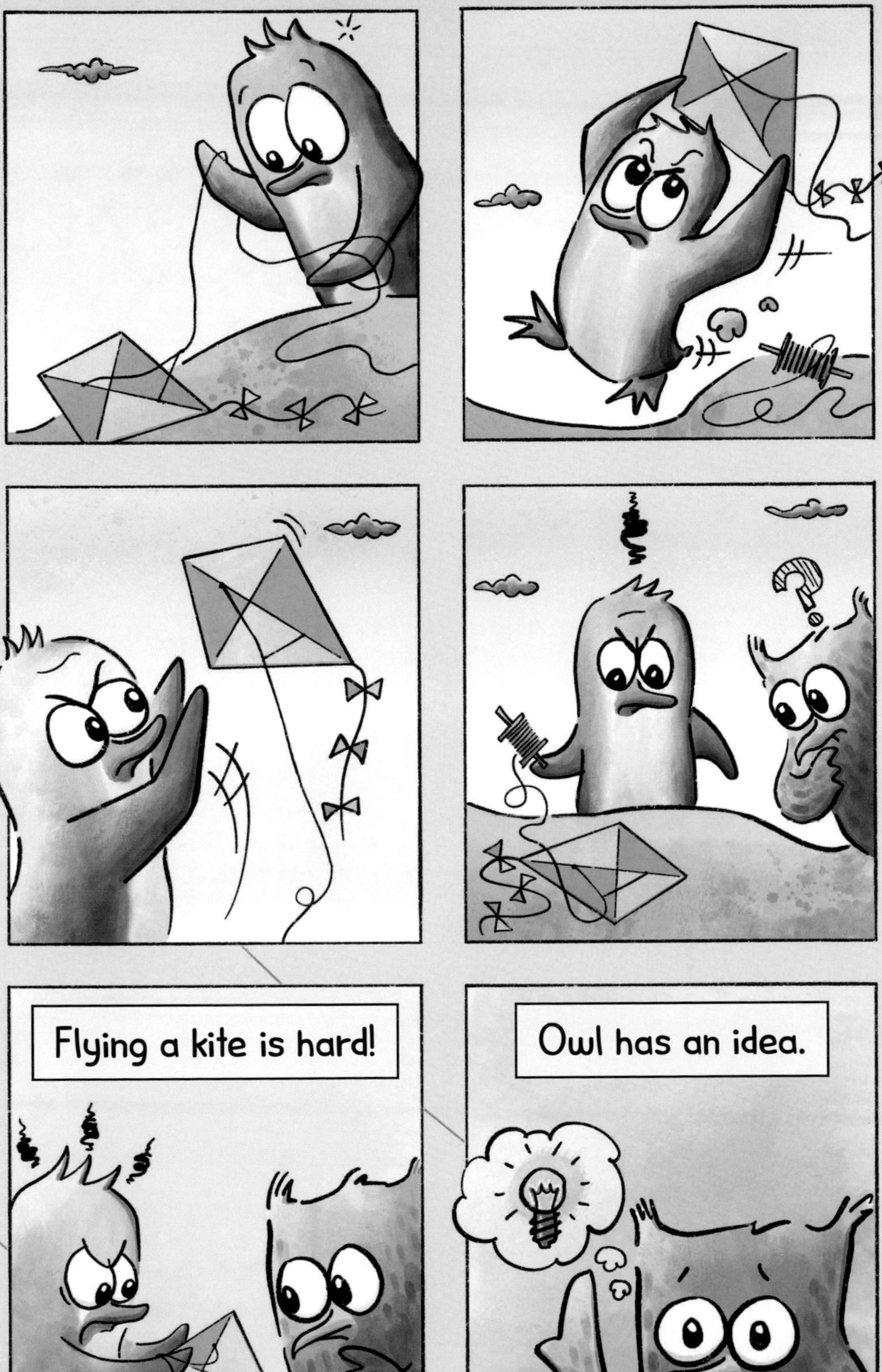
Flying a kite is hard!
Owl has an idea.

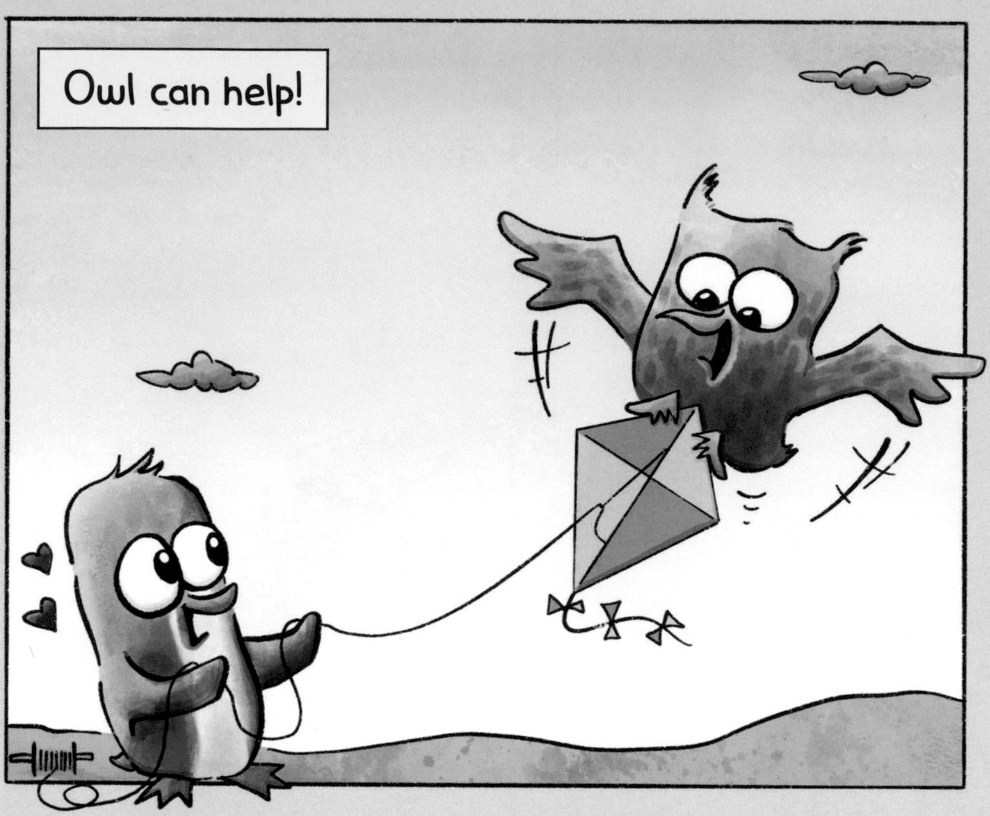
Owl can help!

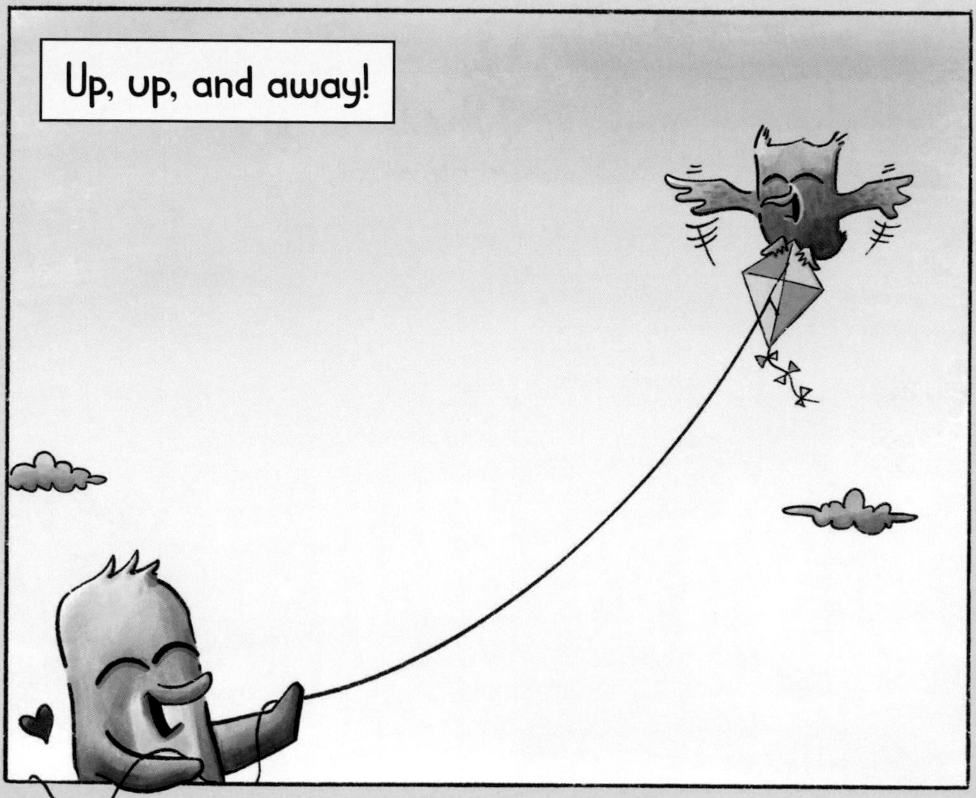
Up, up, and away!

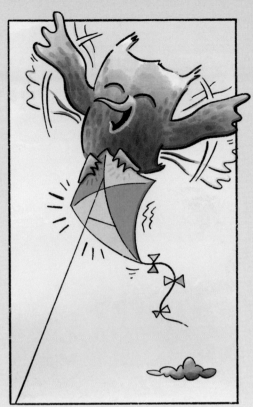

Not so high up!

RIIIIPPP

Owl has another idea!

Owl will be the kite!

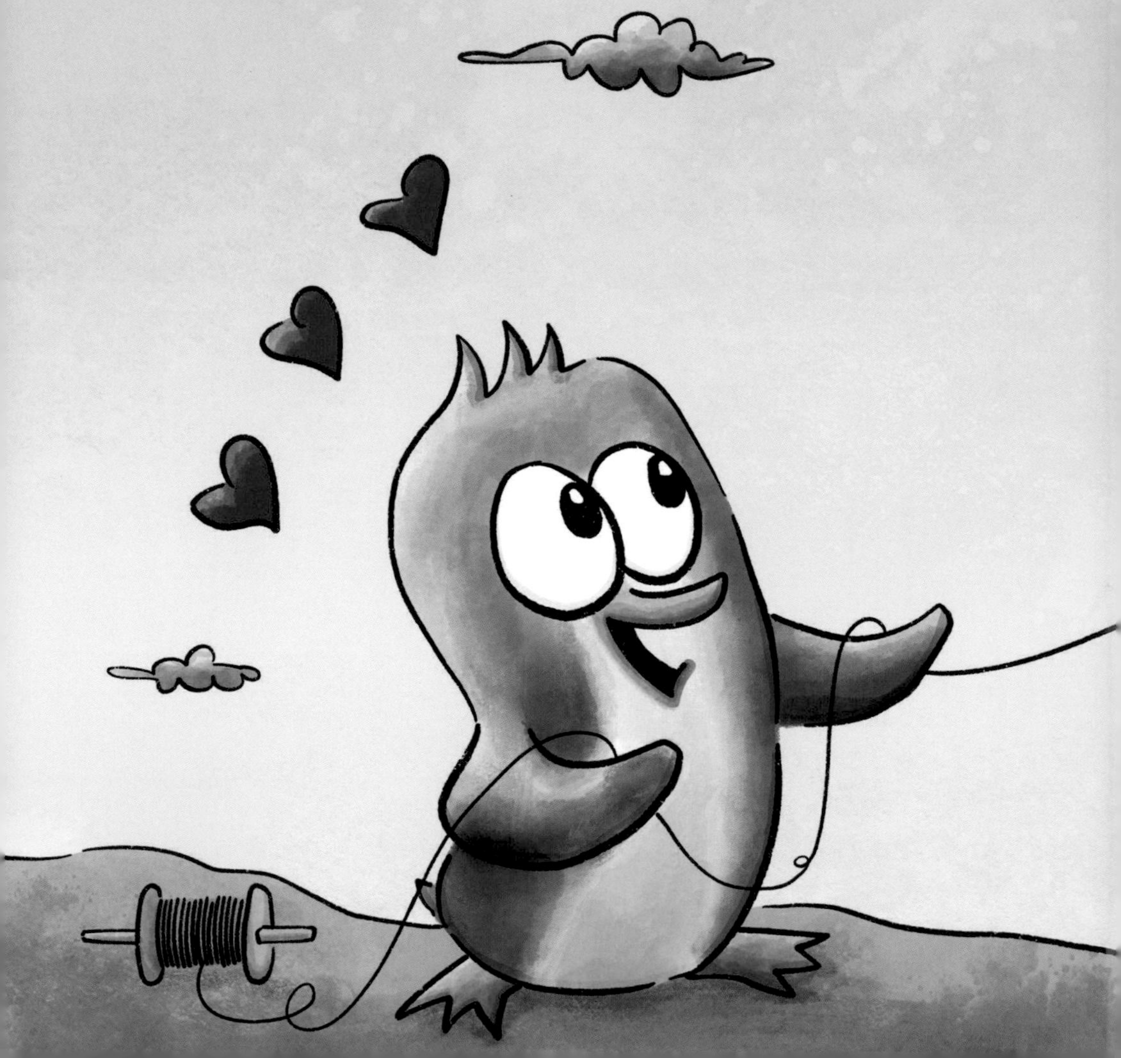

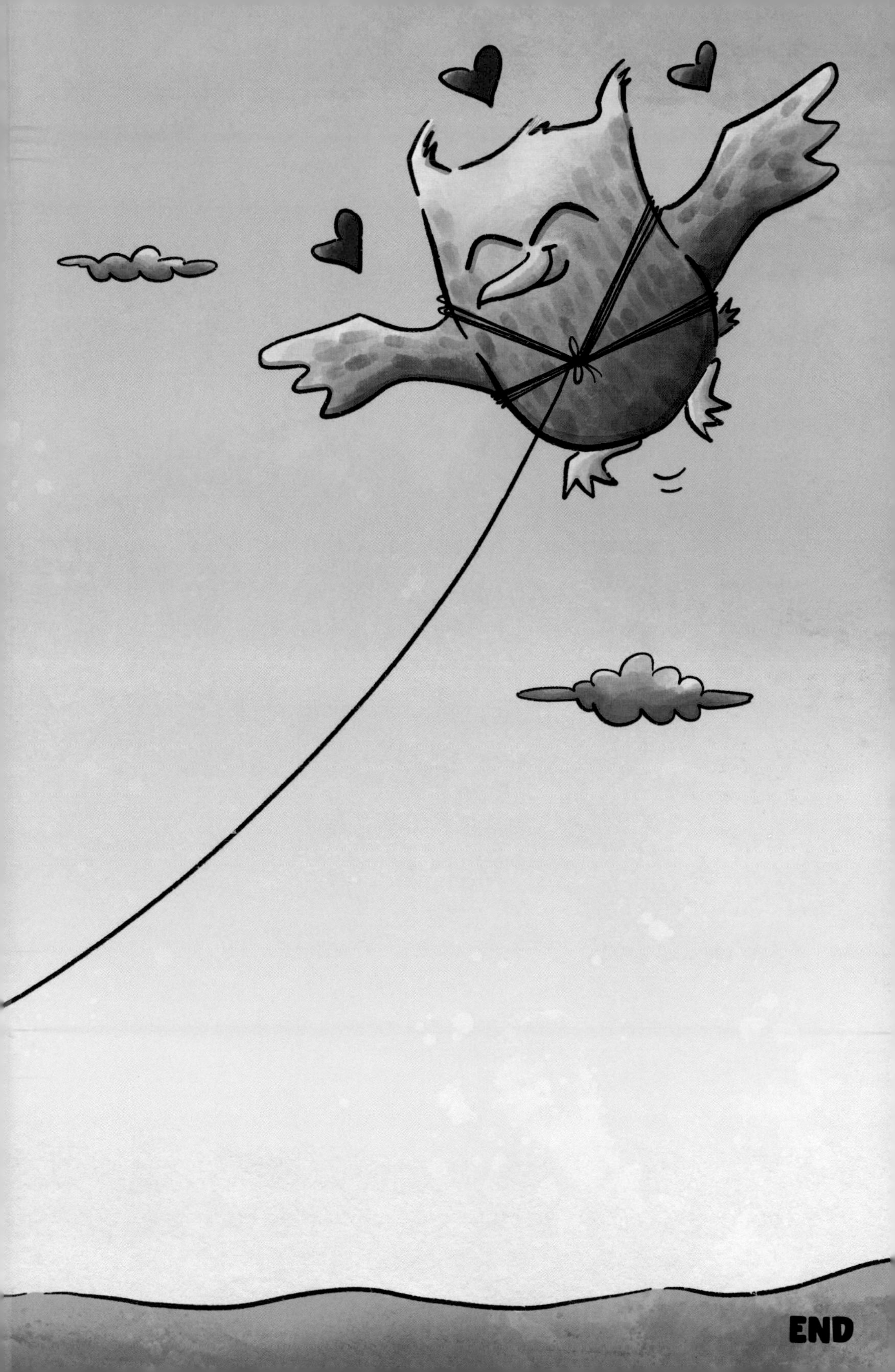
END

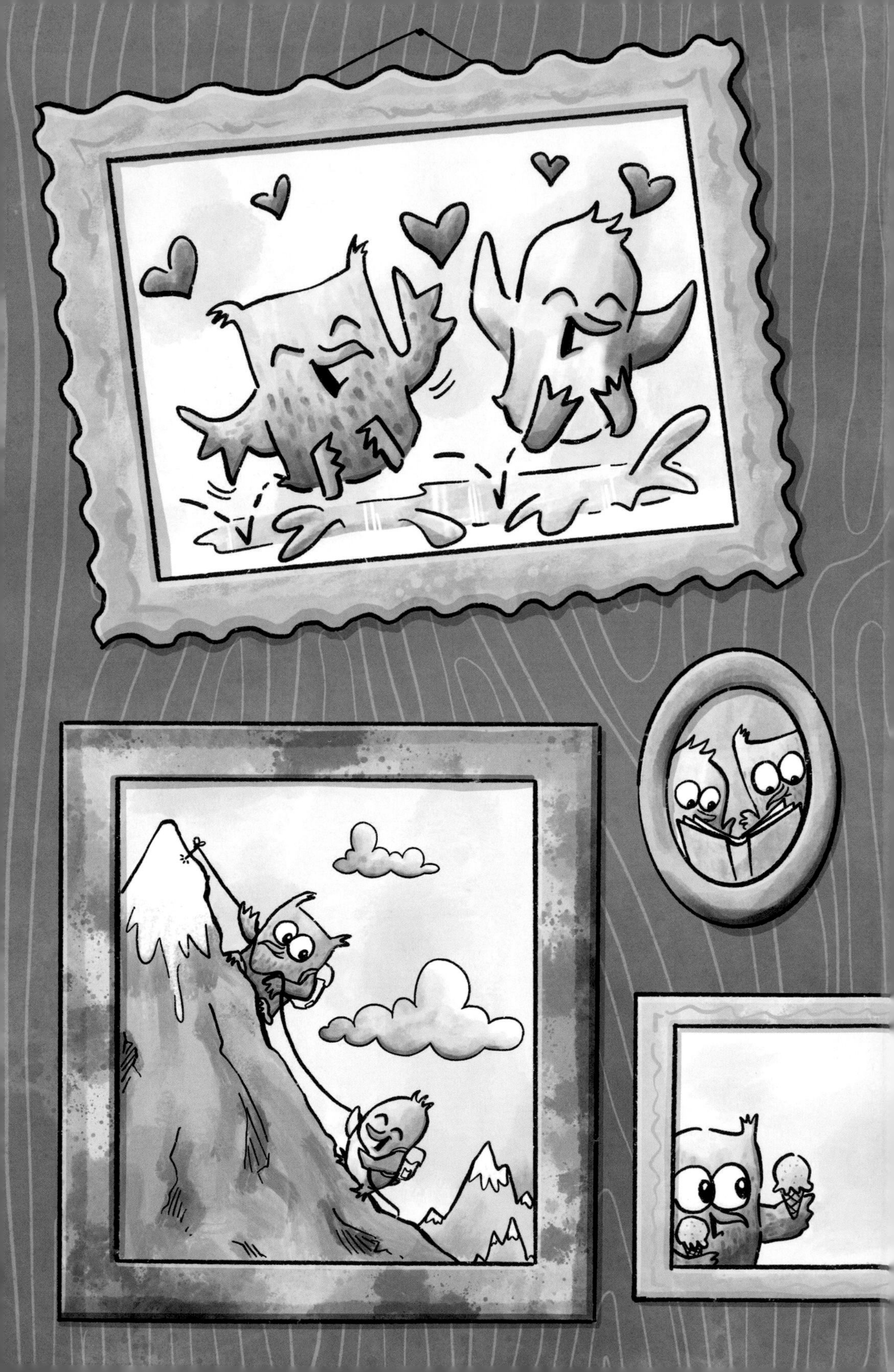